I'm No ANGEL!

BELL STREET SCHOOL

2

HOLLY TATE

Knight Books
Hodder and Stoughton

First published in Great Britain in 1992
by Knight Books.

Typeset by Phoenix Typesetting,
Burley-in-Wharfedale, West Yorks.

British Library C.I.P.

A catalogue record for this book is
available from the British Library

ISBN 0-340-55958-6

Printed and bound in Great Britain
for Hodder and Stoughton Children's
Books, a division of Hodder and
Stoughton Ltd., Mill Road, Dunton
Green, Sevenoaks, Kent TN13 2YA.
(Editorial Office: 47 Bedford Square,
London WC1B 3DP) by
Cox & Wyman Ltd, Reading

1

'What's going on?' asked Emma Pennington, sliding behind her desk. She'd taken some books back to the library and was a few seconds late for registration. And while she was away, something seemed to have happened. The class was buzzing with excitement! 'What have I missed?' she asked Gina Galloway, who was reading one of the blue sheets of paper that everyone seemed to have. 'Is it about the school disco – or Rory Todd?'

Rory Todd was the pop star who was coming to visit Bell Street to make his new video. Maybe his plans had changed. But Gina shook her head. 'It's not about Rory,' she said in her usual bored voice. 'It's just an adventure weekend in Wales. Rock climbing and pony trekking and that sort of thing. I don't understand what everyone's getting so excited about – I've been on lots of activity holidays before.'

Emma could believe that. Gina was the wealthiest girl in the class. In fact she was probably the wealthiest girl in the school. After every holiday she came back and boasted about the exotic places she'd been to and the things she'd done. An activity holiday in Wales would seem pretty tame to her.

It wasn't often that Emma agreed with Gina, but she did about this. She'd hoped the news was going to be really interesting, but instead she just felt disappointed. The others might want to go rock climbing and horse riding, but not her.

At that moment Jamie Thompson stopped by her desk. 'I saved a handout for you,' he said shyly, holding out one of the blue sheets of paper for her.

'I don't need one, thanks,' Emma said coolly.

Jamie looked puzzled. 'Why not?'

'Because I'm not interested,' she replied.

He seemed crestfallen. 'Well, why don't you take it anyway? You might change your mind.' He gave her a nervous lop-sided smile.

Emma didn't really want the handout, but she didn't want to explain why, either. It was easier just to say, 'Okay, if you insist,' and let him put it on her desk. But she knew she wouldn't even bother to read it.

Jamie hesitated, as if he wanted to say something more. Then he changed his mind and went back to his own desk.

Emma felt her face begin to flush. She knew that Jamie liked her – at least that was what the other girls said – but to be honest she found him a bit of an embarrassment. He was nice, and he wasn't bad looking, with his dark hair and big brown eyes. But he wasn't exactly Mr Personality. He'd been at Bell Street school for nearly two terms now and he still hadn't made many friends. Whenever Emma saw him outside class, he seemed to be on his own, reading computer magazines and making drawings for the Design and Technology class. She couldn't help wishing she had someone more exciting as an admirer.

Suddenly Emma realised that her friend Liz Newman, who sat a few desks away, was staring at her with a knowing look. Trust Liz to notice how Jamie had smiled at her! Liz leaned over, as if she was going to say something, but Emma didn't want to hear any comments about Jamie – or the adventure weekend, either. She grabbed the handout and pretended to study it.

The activity centre is near the coast and only a short drive from the mountains of Snowdonia, she found herself reading. *Guests stay in log cabins with bunk beds . . .* As well as more descriptions of the adventure centre there was a list of the activities planned for the weekend. It wasn't all canoeing and rock climbing, Emma noticed. There was going to be a wildlife-watching session, a beach barbecue and songs around the campfire. It sounded like fun.

For a second, Emma wished she could go. But that was just being silly, she reminded herself sternly. Adventure activity weekends weren't for people like her – people with disabilities. How could she go rock climbing or horse riding with her bad leg? You had to be really fit to do things like that, and it was still dangerous. There was no way she could manage it without getting hurt and making a fool of herself.

No, she decided, folding up the handout and putting it in her schoolbag as Miss Tyler began to call the register. No matter how much fun it sounded, she'd better just forget all about the adventure weekend.

'Hey, wait for me!' Becky Burns, the new girl who'd joined the class only a few days ago, came running down the corridor towards Emma and jolted her out of her thoughts.

'I left my bag in the classroom and had to go back for it!' Becky explained with a laugh. 'Liz and all the others have gone on to the art room and I was scared I was going to get lost again.'

Emma smiled. Becky was blonde and bubbly and always getting into scrapes. She hadn't been at Bell Street a whole week, yet already she'd got the class a detention. Even so, Emma liked Becky. She was friendly and funny.

'Are you going on the adventure weekend?' Becky asked as they passed the language lab and pushed open the swing doors leading to the art department. This stretch of corridor had its own special smell of paint and glue and clay that Emma liked.

She shook her head at Becky's question. 'No, I'm not going. I don't do things like that.'

'Why not?' Becky seemed puzzled.

Emma felt startled. Was Becky trying to be funny? 'Because of my leg. I've got a limp. Haven't you noticed?'

Becky looked down at their feet as they walked along. 'It's not a very serious problem, though, is it? Does it hurt?'

Emma was so surprised, she wasn't sure what to say. Most people tried to avoid the subject of her disability, in case they embarrassed her. 'Sometimes it's stiff,' she said. Though not often, she had to admit. 'It used to be really bad. For a long time I had to use sticks to walk. I've had loads of operations to put it right. The doctors have improved it, but they say I'll never be able to walk completely straight,' she explained.

8

Becky listened with her head tilted to one side. 'Liz did tell me you'd been in hospital a lot.'

'Well, Liz knows all about it,' Emma said, nodding. 'She and I were in the same class at junior school. So were Gina and some of the others. They can remember the time I was on sticks and kept going into hospital.' Emma could remember it all clearly, too. Those early schooldays hadn't been very happy. She'd had so much time off that she'd never really had the chance to make close friends or settle down. Just when she began to feel that she belonged at school, she'd have to go back into hospital for a few weeks. And when she returned to the class, Emma always felt like a stranger. It was a feeling that she still carried with her.

'That must be why Liz is always concerned in case you hurt yourself,' Becky mused. 'No wonder she made such a fuss the other day when you fell over.'

'I expect she remembers when I used to fall over and hurt myself a lot,' Emma explained. It suddenly occurred to her that apart from that fall the other day, it had been ages since she'd last had an accident.

'I still don't understand why you don't want to come on the adventure weekend, though,' Becky said, eyeing her curiously.

Emma began to feel irritated. Why did Becky have to keep going on about it? Couldn't she under-stand that someone with a leg like hers just didn't do canoeing and rock climbing? 'I'm no good at things like that,' she said quickly.

'Why not?' Becky seemed surprised. 'I mean, just because you've got a bit of a limp isn't going to stop you from paddling a canoe or sitting on a horse, is it? Why don't you just come along and have some fun with us?'

A bit of a limp? Emma thought indignantly. Becky had no idea! 'Look, I just don't like doing things like that, okay?' Emma insisted as they got to the door of the classroom.

'Okay.' Becky looked apologetic. 'I didn't mean to hurt your feelings. If you don't want to go, that's fine. But it would be nice if everyone in the class came to Wales.'

Emma said nothing. She walked to the far side of the room and found herself a seat. She felt quite upset. No one had talked to her like that before. Becky had obviously never known what it felt like not to be able to walk or run properly. Or how scary it was to stand at the top of a flight of stairs and not know if you could get down them without falling. If she had known, she wouldn't have been so insensitive. Emma held her chin high. How could anyone understand how it felt to be disabled like her?

'Lay the table, one of you. Dinner's nearly ready,' Mrs Pennington called.

Emma glanced across at Andrew, her brother, who was slumped in an armchair watching TV. He didn't move a single muscle. She got up and crossed the wide hallway, with its tiled floor, to the kitchen. Further down the hall the door of her father's study was firmly shut.

Her father was a lawyer and he often brought work back home to the Penningtons' rambling Victorian house. The house was built of red brick, though it was difficult to see the brick for all the ivy that was growing up the walls. Around the house was a large and rather overgrown garden. Some of the kids at school said it was a spooky-looking place, but Emma had lived here all her life and knew there was nothing to be scared of.

The kitchen was cosy and old-fashioned. In fact the whole house was pretty old-fashioned in comparison to the places where Emma's friends lived. Most of the furniture was antique and some of it was a bit threadbare, too. Sometimes Emma couldn't help wishing her parents would buy some bright, modern things instead of stuff from antique shops, but Mr Pennington liked to spend his spare time restoring old furniture.

Emma took four plates from the painted pine dresser and set them out on the big kitchen table. Oscar, the family cat, sat watching her from the windowsill. Emma could hear him purring like a steam engine.

Mrs Pennington carried a dish over from the oven and put it on a mat in the centre. 'I've made chicken casserole this evening.'

'Great,' said Emma, taking cutlery from a drawer. 'Shall I get Dad?'

Mrs Pennington shook her head. 'He's out seeing a client. I'll put his meal in the oven and he can have it later. Where's Andrew?'

As if by magic, Andrew came in, rubbing his eyes. 'Typical,' Emma grumbled. 'When the table needs laying, you can't move. But one whiff of food and you're at the table, waiting for it!'

Andrew pulled out a chair and sat down. 'Behave, child,' he said with a yawn. It always infuriated Emma when he called her a child. He wasn't quite four years older than she was, and he was still at Bell Street school, like her, but he always treated her like a little kid.

'I see you've still got that bit of fluff stuck to your top lip,' Emma retorted, pointing out the moustache he was trying, without much success, to grow. 'It looks like a furry caterpillar.'

Andrew went red. Though he pretended to be so grown-up, he was still self-conscious about his appearance.

'Let's have a ceasefire while we eat, shall we?' Mrs Pennington suggested brightly. 'Will you reach the salt and pepper down for me, Andrew? Your father's put it on the top shelf again.' She pointed up at the top shelf of the dresser.

This was a regular problem. Mr Pennington was very tall and Mrs Pennington was tiny. If she stood on her toes, Emma's mother might just measure five feet tall – but only just. And it wasn't just their height that made Emma's parents different from each other. Her dad liked to take things at a steady pace. Her mum did everything at speed, rushing here and there all the time. Her dad was untidy; her mum liked things to look neat. Her dad drank tea; her mum drank coffee. Her dad liked to wear casual clothes at the weekend; her mum always looked smart. Today, for example, she was wearing a beige skirt and a plain tan-coloured blouse. Emma thought it was amazing that her mum and dad didn't drive each other crazy!

'I had a call from Aunt Edna this morning,' Mrs Pennington said cheerfully, serving the casserole and vegetables. She had a friendly-looking face and short, curly hair, the same chestnut colour as Emma's, except for some grey streaks. 'Her flight from Australia arrives on Monday, so I'm going to meet her at the airport. She'll stay with us for a week or so and then go up to visit Carol in Edinburgh.' Carol was Emma's eldest sister. She was married and living in Scotland. Emma had another big sister, Sally, who was at university.

'Great,' said Andrew, but Emma could tell he didn't really care what was planned for Aunt Ed's visit. He was out almost every night of the week with his friends. He'd be too busy to see much of Aunt Ed. But Emma was looking forward to the visit. It was three years since she'd last seen Aunt Ed, but Emma had really liked her. She was funny and full of life and ideas.

'I wonder whether Aunt Ed'll take me on any more mystery trips?' she smiled. Last time she'd visited, Aunt Ed had taken Emma to the zoo. It wouldn't have mattered, but it was on a day when Emma should have been in school. When Mr Pennington found out, he'd been furious.

Mrs Pennington raised her eyebrows and laughed. 'If Edna suggests any of her madcap ideas, you're to say no!'

'Why?' asked Emma. 'She's fun.'

Mrs Pennington took a deep breath. 'Yes, Aunt Edna is fun, but she doesn't think before she does things. She's too impulsive.'

'Maybe she'll take Emma back to Australia with her,' muttered Andrew, his mouth full. 'Hey, why don't we suggest it?'

'Very funny,' Emma said flatly. 'Anyway, it would

13

be more fun living down-under with Aunt Ed than having to live with *you*.'

'And I suppose I'd miss all the rows we have,' Andrew admitted, finishing his meal and pushing the plate away. 'That was delicious, Mum. The best chicken casserole in the world.' Mrs Pennington lowered her eyelids suspiciously -- and so did Emma. When Andrew paid a compliment, it meant only one thing: he wanted something.

He cleared his throat and put on an innocent-looking expression. 'Mum, some of my friends are planning to go on a cycling tour this summer.'

'Are they really, dear?' Mrs Pennington smiled vaguely at him, as if she couldn't guess what he was going to say next.

'They'll be camping and staying in youth hostels.' Andrew glanced casually at his plate. 'I wondered if I could go with them?'

Mrs Pennington thought about it for a minute. 'Well, your father and I would have to discuss it and we'd want a lot more information about where you were going and who you were going with. But if your plans sound reasonable, yes, I think you're sensible enough to do something like that.'

Emma couldn't believe her ears. Andrew, sensible? That really made her mad. Andrew couldn't be trusted to keep his room tidy or come home on time in the evenings – and yet he was going to be allowed to go off with his friends?

'That's not fair!' she burst out. 'I'm just as sensible as he is!'

Mrs Pennington stared at her in surprise. 'What's unfair, dear?'

14

'You allow Andrew to do what he wants, but when I asked to go to the school disco, you and Dad went on and on for ages about whether it would be safe and what time I'd have to be home,' Emma protested. 'But you're letting him go away on holiday without the slightest fuss!'

'That's because I'm an adult and you're just a child,' Andrew said smugly. 'Anyway, you couldn't go on a cycling holiday if you wanted to – because you can't ride a bike.'

'That's not my fault!' Emma fumed. The only reason she couldn't ride a bicycle was because years ago she'd fallen off the one her parents had given her for Christmas. She hadn't hurt herself badly, but they'd taken her to hospital. When they got back, they locked the bike in the garage so she couldn't use it again.

'Well, if you want to learn to ride a bike, I'll teach you,' Andrew said. Emma was amazed. It was the first time he'd ever offered anything like that. Before she could take him up on it, Mrs Pennington intervened.

'Now you know Emma's not allowed to ride a bicycle,' she said quietly.

'Why not?' Andrew asked. 'Why can't she have a go?'

'You know perfectly well why. It's not safe.'

Andrew shrugged as he turned to Emma. 'See, it's not me being unfair.' Then he glanced up at the clock on the kitchen wall. 'Hey, I've got to dash – I said I'd meet the team for football practice at six thirty.' He scraped his chair noisily as he got up.

Mrs Pennington began to carry the dishes to the

sink. 'Would you give me a hand with these, dear?' she asked. Emma wrinkled her nose. Right now she didn't feel in the mood for being helpful. Maybe she should take a leaf out of Andrew's book and just be lazy and irresponsible. The problem was, she didn't know how!

Mrs Pennington noticed her silence. She leant across the table with a sympathetic expression. 'I know that sometimes things don't seem fair to you,' she said softly, 'but Andrew is older than you. And we worry so much more about you. We don't want you taking any risks. Try and remember that. We have to be tough because we care about you.'

Emma sighed. When her mother put it like that, it was difficult to be angry. She was really lucky to have parents who cared enough to worry about her. But if it was true and she was so lucky, how come she still felt so annoyed?

2

As Emma arrived at school the next morning, it began to rain. She hurried indoors with everyone else and stood in the main entrance, shaking the drops from her dark hair and the navy sweatshirt she always wore. Some of the other girls wore ordinary clothes, but Mrs Pennington was strict about school uniform. She always insisted on Emma wearing the official school sweatshirt. Emma didn't really mind. After all, the sweatshirt was quite smart.

Miss Tyler, resplendent in a bright red jacket and matching scarlet lipstick, was standing by the entrance and instructing students where to wait until the bell rang for registration. 'You can wait in the hall or go to 2K's form room and wait outside,' she told Emma.

Emma looked into the crowded hall where most students were waiting. She could see the back of Liz Newman's head, her hair neatly held back in its velvet band. Maybe she'd go and talk to Liz – but then her eye fell on Becky Burns, standing next to Liz. After what Becky had said the previous day, Emma didn't feel like chatting to her. She'd go and wait outside the form room.

When she got there she found a lone figure wearing a red baseball jacket waiting by the door. Though his face was hidden behind the pages of a magazine, she knew who it was: Jamie Thompson. *Just my luck*, thought Emma. She thought about going back to the hall, but he looked up as she approached and gave her his usual lop-sided smile. 'Hi, Emma,' he said shyly.

It was too late to turn round now. She couldn't be so rude. 'Hi, Jamie.' She unzipped her bag and pulled out the book she was reading for her English project. Maybe they could both stand there reading and she wouldn't have to chat to him. It wasn't that she minded talking to Jamie, but if other people saw them together, they might jump to the wrong conclusion. As she pulled out the book, a sheet of pale blue paper fluttered to the floor. Jamie bent down to pick it up.

'I see you kept the adventure weekend handout,' he said, handing it to her. He sounded pleased. Emma felt embarrassed. She thought she'd thrown the handout away. Now Jamie might think she'd kept it because he'd given it to her! 'Have you changed your mind about going to Wales?' he asked.

Emma shook her head. 'No. How about you – are you going?'

Jamie suddenly looked gloomy. 'Yes – worse luck. I don't really want to go but my parents think it'll be a good idea. They say the activities will do me good and I'll make friends. That's all they go on about, making friends.' He smiled wistfully. 'They say they want me to go for my own good.'

Emma couldn't help grinning. 'My parents say that to me sometimes – usually when they *don't* want me to do something! When I asked if I could go to the disco they said no at first. My mum said it was for my own good. But I managed to talk them round.'

'I wish my parents were like that.' Jamie sighed. 'At least yours don't try and push you into things you don't want to do. Your parents wouldn't force me to go on this adventure weekend, would they?'

'No – I don't suppose so.' Emma frowned, feeling suddenly confused. No one had ever envied her her parents before! She knew that people like Liz thought Mr and Mrs Pennington were pretty strict. They said no to Emma's plans more often than they said yes. They'd said no to swimming lessons and no when she'd asked if she could go on a sponsored walk for charity. And they'd be bound to say no to this adventure weekend, even if Emma wanted to go.

The more she thought about it, the more she disagreed with Jamie. 'You might think my parents sound great,' she said slowly, 'but they don't let me do any of the things I want to do. I'd prefer parents like yours.'

Jamie looked surprised. 'You *wouldn't*. My parents don't mind what happens to me, so long as I do everything they want me to do.'

Emma frowned. 'Sometimes I think *my* mum and dad would like it if they could just wrap me up in cotton wool for ever.'

'Well, I wouldn't mind being wrapped up instead of being packed off to Wales to abseil on a rope down a cliff,' Jamie replied quickly. 'You don't realise how lucky you are!'

That irritated Emma. If Jamie were in her shoes, he wouldn't think she was so lucky. She stared at him squarely. 'Well I think you're the lucky one.'

She said it with a smile, but she was surprised by just how angry she felt. What right had Jamie Thompson to complain? She was the one who had all the problems.

There will be a choice of activities including canoeing, pony trekking, rock climbing, abseiling, mountain biking, archery, wildlife tracking and observation and orienteering. Evening activities will include a barbecue and disco on the beach and songs and storytelling around the campfire . . .

Sitting in the library during lunch break, Emma read the handout for about the hundredth time. And every time she read it, she wanted to go to Wales just a little bit more.

The more she thought about it, the more certain she felt that she could manage the weekend without making a fool of herself. Jamie's attitude had really made her think. He didn't seem to appreciate how lucky he was to be one hundred per cent fit, or to have parents who let him try things. And the more annoyed Emma felt about that, the more she remembered Becky Burns's comment about her leg not preventing her from horse riding or canoeing.

Maybe when she'd said that, Becky wasn't being insensitive. Maybe she really did have a point. After all, Emma reasoned, once she'd climbed into the canoe or got up on the horse, who would guess that she had a limp? And the same went for abseiling. She felt pretty sure that it wouldn't matter a bit. Rock climbing might be a bit more difficult if her hip was stiff, but she probably wouldn't have to do all the activities. And they wouldn't make her do anything she really couldn't manage, would they?

The instructors wouldn't want her to hurt herself any more than she did!

Emma could feel her stomach beginning to flutter with excitement. It was a bit scary, too, to think of herself actually doing things like canoeing and abseiling. But the more she allowed herself to imagine it, the more possible it seemed.

It was crazy, but she felt as if something amazing had happened to her in the past few hours. It was as if a barrier that she'd always assumed was there had been taken down. All these years she'd just taken it for granted that sports and activities weren't for people like her! But why not? Maybe they'd be fun. Maybe she'd hate them and never want to ride a horse or go canoeing again. But she'd never know if she didn't take the risk and try them, would she? Emma smiled secretly to herself. It was going to be great!

But suddenly she returned to earth with a bump. *She* might have made up her mind to go on the activity holiday, but that was the easy bit. The hardest part of all was telling her parents. And what were they going to say about the weekend in Wales?

Emma heard her parents open the front door and come clattering down the tiled hall. They'd been out to do the weekly shopping at the supermarket. Her father normally didn't like Saturday morning crowds, but today he was whistling as he carried the bags down the hall. That was always a good sign. He must be in a really good mood. This was the perfect opportunity.

She dashed back to her bedroom and picked up

the pale blue handout, then ran down the stairs. Her father was unpacking something wrapped in old newspaper.

'Hello, love!' Mr Pennington smiled as Emma came in and planted a kiss on her forehead. He was like a big bear, tall and cuddly. Well, Emma thought he was cuddly, though her mum sometimes accused him of being overweight. Even his hair was golden-brown, like a teddy bear's. Right now, he was looking really pleased and his eyes were twinkling.

'What have you got there?' Emma asked curiously.

'We went to the market to buy fruit and vegetables,' her father explained, snipping the string with the kitchen scissors, 'and I found a stall selling bits and pieces of furniture and paintings.'

'You mean a junk stall,' said Emma.

'Bric-a-brac,' corrected her mother, who was putting groceries in the cupboards.

'Collectors' items,' Mr Pennington insisted indignantly. 'Have a look at this. It's not junk.' He unwrapped the last layer of paper and revealed a dusty painting of a landscape.

'Mmmm,' said Emma, trying to sound appreciative. To be honest, the picture looked pretty boring.

'Okay.' Her father laughed, seeing her face. 'Maybe you don't like it much. But I hope you'll like this a bit more.' He handed her a paper bag.

Emma opened it. It was the latest Rory Todd cassette, *Today is the Day*, which she'd wanted to buy for weeks. 'Thanks!' She flung her arms round his neck and kissed him.

Mr Pennington smiled. 'Well, you've been helping

to get Aunt Ed's room ready for her, so I thought you deserved a reward.'

'I've just made up the bed and dusted. I want it to be nice for her when she gets here.' Emma hopped nervously from foot to foot. She wanted to go and listen to the tape, but there was something she had to do first. 'Dad, the class at school are going on an activity holiday,' Emma said quickly. She gave him the handout.

Mrs Pennington looked up. 'Is it like the activity course Sally went on? She did pottery and sculpture and jewellery-making and that kind of thing. I always wished I'd been able to go, too!'

'No!' Mr Pennington exclaimed in surprise as he read the information. 'It's not that kind of activity holiday at all. It's canoeing and mountain biking and pot-holing—'

'There's no pot-holing, Dad!' Emma protested. 'It's just things like pony trekking and abseiling.'

'Abseiling? Isn't that where you come down a cliff backwards on a rope?' Mrs Pennington stopped putting the groceries away.

'Yes,' said Emma, trying to gauge how shocked her parents were. 'I know it *sounds* dangerous but Gina Galloway's done it before and she says it's really safe. You wear a safety harness and there are two ropes in case one breaks . . . '

Mrs Pennington arched her eyebrows in alarm. 'You're not saying that you really want to go and do this, are you, Emma?'

'Well . . . ' She looked at her toes and tried to summon some of the bravery and excitement she'd felt yesterday. 'Yes. I'd like to try riding and canoeing—'

23

'But you can't even swim!' cut in Mr Pennington, looking confused.

'Only because you didn't want me to learn,' Emma reminded him, feeling annoyed. 'Anyway, they'll have life jackets. And the water isn't very deep. Liz Newman was scared because she can't swim either, but Miss Tyler told her there was nothing to worry about.'

Mrs Pennington closed the cupboard door. For a moment there was a tense silence. Then she shook her head.

'What's come over you, Emma? You don't like doing things like this! What's made you suddenly decide you want to go horse riding and rock climbing?'

Emma bit her lip. This wasn't going to be easy, she could tell from her parents' expressions. 'I just thought I'd like to try some of these things for a change. I've never done anything really exciting before.'

Her father gave one of his huge sighs. 'Come and sit down,' he said, drawing out a chair at the kitchen table. Instead of being carefree and happy, as he'd been a few minutes ago, he was serious and straight-faced. Emma obediently sat down. 'I know you want to go on this holiday,' he began, 'but these activities are far too dangerous for you.'

Emma had guessed he'd say that, and she was prepared. 'If they're so dangerous, they wouldn't allow the school to send us on this holiday,' she argued.

Mr Pennington nodded and ran his fingers through his hair. 'For most of your classmates this kind of thing is fine. But you're different, Emma. You're more delicate than the others. You've got to remember that. You can't risk hurting yourself.'

'That's right.' Mrs Pennington put her arm round Emma's shoulder and gave her a little hug. 'Remember all the time you spent in hospital. If you had an accident you might end up with a bad limp again. Think how awful that would be.'

'But I'll be careful,' Emma promised. 'I don't want to get hurt; I just want to join in with everyone else.'

Her father smiled sympathetically. 'It's not worth the risk. If something bad happened, we'd never forgive ourselves for letting you go.'

'Will you just think about it?' Emma pleaded, feeling like crying. 'When Andrew asked to go on his cycling trip the other day, you said you'd give it your consideration. You're not even going to think about this.'

Mrs Pennington wrinkled her forehead. She looked more worried than Emma could remember. 'But Andrew's older than you are and he doesn't have a disability. You have to accept that you're different – and we have to be much more careful with you because of that.'

Emma shook her head in disbelief. She didn't have a chance of success. Both of them had already made up their minds against her. 'You never let me do anything I want to do!' she complained.

'That's not true,' insisted her father. 'We've said you can go to the school disco, haven't we? But it would be irresponsible of us to let you go on this holiday. We can't do it.'

Mrs Pennington gave her another squeeze. 'We

only want what's best for you, dear, but that doesn't include rock climbing and canoeing. If there's some other holiday you want to go on, one with less dangerous activities, I promise we'll let you go.'

'But I want to go on this one!' Emma's voice broke with sobs, even though she tried to hold them back. 'It'll be all right. I'm not made of glass, you know!'

Her father sighed again, and this time she could tell he was beginning to lose patience. 'I don't want to have to be strict with you, Emma, but it's out of the question. The sooner you forget about going to Wales, the less difficult it will be for you.'

He held out the sheet of paper with the activity holiday details. 'It says here that you need the signature of your parents or a responsible adult on the slip at the bottom of this handout, giving their permission for you to go. And neither of us will be signing it.'

He got up and picked up the picture from the market. 'I think there's a good place for this in the hall,' he said, and went off. As far as he was concerned, Emma thought, that was that.

But she still hadn't given up hope. 'Mum, please, think about it,' she begged.

Her mother ignored the plea. 'Has someone been encouraging you to go on this weekend? Is it Miss Tyler?'

'No,' Emma insisted. 'I just want to try something new for a change.'

Mrs Pennington didn't seem convinced. 'Well if anyone *is* encouraging you to do this sort of thing, don't listen to them. We know what's best for you, Emma. Trust us. We have more experience of these things than you do.'

*

How could they know what was really best for her? Emma thought as she sat upstairs in her bedroom. Her parents treated her like a baby! They were never going to let her live her own life. She might get to twenty or thirty or even forty years old and they'd still be trying to tell her that they knew best.

Then she caught sight of her face in the mirror above her desk. Her eyes were huge and shining and her cheeks were red from crying. She looked like a helpless baby. No wonder no one took her seriously.

And maybe, Emma mused as she wiped away the tears, her parents were right. Perhaps she *was* too young to know what was good for her. After all, they were her parents. They wouldn't deliberately want to do anything to hurt her. If she couldn't depend on them to make the right decisions for her, who could she trust?

That was it. She'd got over-excited by the things Becky had said. She'd been carried away by the thought of the adventure holiday. But Emma must have been dreaming if she'd imagined she could ever go abseiling, or manage a canoe. She'd just end up with everyone laughing at her efforts.

Emma dried her eyes and sighed. Thank goodness her parents were more sensible than she was. They'd saved her from making a real fool of herself!

3

Jasmine Scott held out the latest edition of *The Look*, a fashion magazine. 'I want a pair of leggings just like that,' she announced, chewing away on her gum. 'Aren't they just fabulous?'

Emma looked at the photograph. 'But they're nearly thirty pounds!' she exclaimed.

Jas giggled. She had very dark cropped hair and eyes the colour of bitter chocolate, and when she laughed she looked like a naughty pixie. 'I wasn't planning on that pair exactly, but I've seen some cheaper ones in a boutique in the shopping centre.'

'I don't think I'll be buying a pair,' Liz Newman said rather primly, looking up from her history assignment, which she was just reading through. 'The colours all clash! Red and orange and pink – we'll need to wear sunglasses when you've got them on.'

Emma agreed with Liz. Bright leggings weren't really Liz's style. She usually wore plain, neat clothes. Today, for example, she was wearing a pretty white blouse with blue embroidery around the collar, and a navy skirt that came just above her knees, with navy blue tights. Emma looked down at her own legs, clad in navy socks. She wished she could wear tights, but her mother said they weren't practical for school, they'd keep laddering.

And her shoes weren't right, either. They were just plain lace-ups. Jas was wearing Doc Martens, which looked good with her short skirt. And even Liz had smart loafers. Emma had tried to persuade her mother to buy her a pair, but Mrs Pennington would only look at boring old lace-ups. She said they'd be easier for Emma to walk in. Emma couldn't see that they made any difference. All they did was make her look different from everyone else.

'Hey, I nearly forgot. Look what I've got.' Liz undid her bag. Inside it, everything was tucked away neatly in pockets and coloured folders. Everything Liz did was organised. She unzipped a pocket and pulled out a little glass pot. 'It's lip gloss.' She unscrewed the lid and smoothed some on her lips. 'My mum let me buy it on Saturday. She won't let me wear proper lipstick but she says this is all right because it stops your lips getting cracked.'

'Let me try some!' Jas dipped a finger in the pot. 'Mmm, strawberry flavour! It's lovely.'

'Try some, Emma.' Liz held out the pot. 'Don't worry, it's not very bright. Miss Tyler'll never know you've got it on.'

Emma hesitated. It was against school rules to wear make-up, though lots of the girls did.

'We know you're an angel and you never break school rules,' said Jas, as if she'd read Emma's mind. 'But just try it. You can always wipe it off.'

Emma frowned. Why did everyone assume that she was a goody-two-shoes? She dipped a fingertip in and smoothed the gloss over her lips.

'That looks great!' Liz grinned. 'The colour really suits you.'

'Yeah,' Jas agreed. 'It makes you look just a bit more grown-up.' She flicked the pages of the fashion magazine. 'You know, something like this would really suit you. It would look great with the red-coloured glints in your hair.' She pointed to a silk top in a warm apricot colour. 'If you wore that and a smudge of matching eyeshadow, you'd look really good.' She peered hard at Emma. 'You know, you've got the longest, darkest eyelashes I've ever seen! Are you sure they're not false?'

'No!' Emma blushed with embarrassment. Not just because of what Jas had said about her eyelashes, but because everyone was looking at her – including Becky, who'd just joined them. Emma felt really self-conscious. Usually when people looked at her it was because of her limp. They stared for a bit and then looked away, feeling sorry for her. She wished they'd all talk about something else, instead of putting the spotlight on her. She didn't know about things like make-up and hair styles, not like the rest of them. Compared to her they all seemed so sophisticated.

Emma jumped to her feet. 'I've got to go and find Mr Nicholson to tell him about . . . ' She didn't finish the sentence. She just picked up her bag and set off across the grass towards the library like a startled rabbit. But she hadn't noticed that the bag's shoulder strap had come undone. As she walked away it caught round her ankle and sent her flying – straight into Gina Galloway, who was standing with a couple of her friends.

'Aagh!' cried Gina, brushing strands of her hair out of her eyes, 'Do you have to be so clumsy? Look what you've done.' Gina had been holding an opened carton of orange juice. When Emma had bumped into her, some of the juice had squirted on to Gina's shirt.

'I'm sorry!' Emma tried to mop up the juice with a tissue from her pocket, but it didn't seem to do much good. She could feel her face getting hotter and hotter with embarrassment.

'Oh, leave it,' Gina muttered crossly. 'It'll have to go to the dry cleaners tomorrow. It's silk – you can't just put it in the washing-machine, you know.'

'I'm really sorry,' Emma repeated. 'I tripped—'

'It's okay, it's okay.' Gina waved a hand as if it didn't matter. 'You can't help it, Emma, I know.'

Emma felt really humiliated. She was suddenly aware that almost everyone in the playground was staring at her. She could feel Liz and Becky's eyes boring into her back. They must think she was really stupid, racing off like that just because Jas had commented on her looks. And she *would* have to trip over, too! Emma hurried across the playground wishing that she was invisible. To think that on Friday she'd convinced herself that she'd be able to manage abseiling and horse riding – when the truth was, she could hardly even walk straight!

She scurried across the main playground and round the corner of the science block, to the smaller playground at the back of the school. This area wasn't so popular. It didn't get any sunshine and there was no grass, just a couple of old benches to sit on.

Up ahead, sitting on a bench with his back turned towards her and his face buried in a book, was Jamie Thompson. Emma sat down on the low brick wall

31

and hoped he wouldn't look up and see her. There was nowhere else for her to go. She couldn't go into school, not until the bell rang. And she couldn't go out to the main playground again.

She stole a glance at Jamie. Why was he always on his own? she wondered. There was nothing wrong with him. It seemed strange that he hadn't made any friends yet. She supposed he was just a bit of an outsider. A misfit.

A bit like her, really, Emma realised with a sinking heart. She'd never thought of herself that way before, but it was true. She just didn't seem to fit in with the other girls in 2K. They all talked about pop stars and music and clothes and boyfriends, while she – well, sometimes she didn't say a word when she was with them. She didn't really belong with them, and she never had. If she hadn't spent so much time on her own in hospital when she was younger, maybe it wouldn't be so difficult to fit in now.

And what had Jas said about her being an angel? That was part of the problem. They were nice to her, but somehow they treated her as if she was different from the rest of them. If it wasn't for her leg and her parents treating her like a baby, she might have a chance of fitting in. But she was different. Emma gave a deep sigh. And no one could do anything about her leg, so it looked as if she was always going to be different.

'Come on, girls. Hurry up and change into your kit.' The P.E. teacher strode into the changing-room, clapping her hands.

'Where's Mrs Fry?' asked Gina Galloway. Mrs Fry

was their usual gym teacher, who was short and blond, with muscles that would make a strong man jealous. The gym teacher who'd just walked in was tall and thin, and not very friendly-looking.

'Mrs Fry has strained her back and is having a few days off work. I'm Miss Dowling and I'll be taking gym class while she's away.' There were giggles all around the changing-room at the news.

'Fancy Fitness-Freak Fry hurting her back!' exclaimed Charlie Farrel, tying back her long red hair in one of the scarves she always wore. When she'd finished she took off her wire-framed glasses and put them safely in her bag. 'Maybe Mrs Fry tried lifting something that was a bit too heavy for her – like a shop,' she suggested.

'Or a bus,' Becky said with a laugh as she bent down to tie her shoes.

'No, Mrs Fry could lift a bus easily,' Liz said with a straight face. 'It would have to be something much bigger than that!'

Emma sat in her usual spot on the end of the bench and listened to them joking. Miss Dowling turned around and spotted her. 'Come on, the others are almost ready. Where's your kit?' she asked.

'I don't do gym,' Emma explained. 'I never do. I've got a bad leg.'

Miss Dowling wrinkled her brow. 'Can you walk on it? Did you walk to the gym?'

'Yes,' Emma said, puzzled, 'but I usually stay here in the changing room or go to the library and read while the others—' But Miss Dowling wasn't listening.

'Does your leg hurt you?' she asked quickly.

'No,' Emma admitted. 'But I can't—' Half the heads in the changing-room had swivelled to listen in on the conversation.

'No buts,' said Miss Dowling, cutting Emma short before she could go into details. She went over to the cupboard where the spare gym kits and lost property were kept and pulled out a white T-shirt and a pair of track suit bottoms. 'You can change into these.'

Emma was speechless. She took the gym kit and just sat there, unsure what to do. She'd never done gym before, ever. Her parents had written to the school and asked for her to be allowed to sit out the lesson. Mrs Fry had never tried to make her take part. Her head whirled with confusion.

'But Miss Dowling, Emma isn't allowed . . . ' It was Liz Newman who'd spoken up. She looked really worried.

'There's a first time for everything.' Miss Dowling compressed her lips into a straight line. 'Everybody needs exercise, even people who have trouble with their legs. We'll see what Emma can do.' She gave a little smile. 'Don't worry, I'm not going to ask you to do somersaults on the trampoline. If you find it's too difficult, you can sit it out.'

Emma had the distinct feeling that she wasn't going to have much choice. She bent down and began to untie her shoes. Her hands were shaking and she had trouble with the laces.

'The rest of you can go into the gym. We're playing volleyball this afternoon,' Miss Dowling announced. Some of the girls cheered, but Emma gulped and felt fear tightening her chest. She had no idea how to play volleyball.

Liz gave her an encouraging smile as she walked into the gym a few minutes later. The first match was already in progress and Miss Dowling was busy refereeing it. Liz and Becky quickly explained the rules. 'It's easy,' Becky said. 'All you have to do is knock the ball over the net and make it hit the ground on your opponents' side. They keep hitting it back at you, but you mustn't let it touch the ground.'

It sounded simple enough, but it didn't look that easy to Emma. Mina Stevens threw herself across the floor to hit the ball at one point, and landed with a terrible thud. Emma winced – and so did Liz. 'You don't have to do that,' Liz whispered.

'Thanks for telling me,' Emma whispered back.

Eventually Miss Dowling blew her whistle and the first set of players came off the court and sat on the sidelines. 'Right, let's have another two teams.' She divided them up and Emma found herself walking on to the court with Liz, Becky, Jas, Charlie and Lucy Groves.

She took her position by the net, feeling terrified. On the other side Gina Galloway was bouncing around to warm up. Her hair bobbed up and down like a big blob of floaty yellow candy floss. 'You haven't got a hope!' she called out to Liz. But Liz seemed more worried about Emma than about winning.

'Just take it gently,' Liz advised. 'Don't try running around too much.'

Emma nodded. Although she felt reassured by what Liz said, she also felt a bit annoyed. She wasn't made of glass, after all. She might not be able to run as fast as the others or dive after the ball, but she wasn't going to fall apart. At least, she hoped not. Her mind flicked back to that morning, when she'd tripped into Gina, and she felt a shiver of fear.

But there was no time to think about it. 'Play!' called Miss Dowling and the ball came sailing over the net directly towards Emma. Emma saw it coming, balled her fist, stepped forward and knocked it back as hard as she could. It sailed up over the net and bounced just out of Gina's reach.

'Yes!' Jas yelled and slapped her on the back. 'You've played this before, haven't you?'

Emma shook her head, hardly able to believe what had happened.

'Just a fluke. Beginner's luck,' Gina said sourly.

Jas curled her lip. 'You're such a good sport, Gina,' she taunted sarcastically.

'Was that all right?' Emma asked, turning to Liz. It had happened so quickly, she wasn't sure what she'd done. Gina was probably right. Her shot had been down to luck more than skill.

'Yes, of course it was!' Liz was looking at her in complete surprise, as if she'd expected her to be knocked flat by the ball. Emma took a deep breath. The butterflies were back in her stomach, but they felt great! She'd scored, and she was still standing up!

And she managed to stay on her feet all through the match, even when she had to lunge after a low ball that Gina angled at her. When Miss Dowling blew the final whistle and announced that Liz's team had won, Emma could hardly believe it.

'Well done, team,' Liz said with a beaming smile. 'Emma, you were great!'

'Look at Gina's face,' Charlie said with a grin. 'She looks as if she's sucking a lemon.'

Gina pushed past them on the way back to the changing-room. 'Don't look so pleased with yourselves,' she said, scowling. 'We weren't giving it our best. We let you win because of your handicap.' And she stared pointedly at Emma.

'Don't take any notice of her. She's the world's worst loser,' Becky retorted, her blue eyes glittering with anger.

'They were playing their hearts out,' Jas agreed. She pulled a pack of chewing-gum out of her bag, taking care not to let the teacher see it. 'Want some?' she asked Emma.

Gum wasn't allowed in school, though Jas didn't seem to take much notice of the rule. She was always chewing away. Emma hesitated for a second, then took a piece and popped it into her mouth, feeling really wicked. But why shouldn't she? After all, she wasn't supposed to do gym class, and look how well that had turned out!

Miss Dowling came over while they were changing back into uniform. 'Emma, would you take your kit home and wash it?' she asked. 'Bring it to the next gym class and it can go back into the cupboard.' Emma nodded. It was difficult to speak with chewing-gum in her mouth. She felt really guilty. 'You've got good coordination,' Miss Dowling went on. 'If we can make you a bit more confident about running around, you could be a good player.'

Emma couldn't believe her ears. She was just pleased because she hadn't fallen over and made a fool of herself. And now they were saying that she might be good at volleyball! Miss Dowling turned away, then swung back. 'Oh, and Emma, you know you're not allowed to chew gum in school. Would you put it in the bin, please? And don't do it again.'

Emma felt as if her face was on fire. She wrapped the gum in its paper and took it over to the bin. It felt like a hundred miles across the changing-room floor.

Liz stared wide-eyed as Emma began to pull on her socks and shoes. 'I can't believe it!' she said, shaking her head. 'I never thought I'd see the day when Emma Pennington was caught chewing gum in school!'

Becky, who was sitting next to Emma, laughed as she brushed her blond hair and fastened it in its silver clip. 'Maybe this is the start of a life of crime!'

Emma giggled, though her heart was still racing from the shock of being told off by Miss Dowling. 'I know you all think I'm an angel,' she said shyly, 'but I'm not, you know. And I don't want to be.'

'Good,' said Becky, tossing back her hair. 'Because being an angel is no fun at all!' They all laughed.

Charlie was polishing her glasses. She leaned over as she put them on. 'Liz and Becky are coming back to my house after school. Do you want to come too?'

There was nothing that Emma would have liked more. But she couldn't. 'I've got to go straight home. My Aunt Ed's come from Australia and my mum asked me to get back in time for tea.'

'Aunt Ed?' Becky laughed. 'She sounds more like an uncle to me.'

'She's Aunt Edna, really, but she doesn't like her name,' Emma explained. 'She was a tomboy when she was young, so everyone called her Ed.'

'She sounds nice,' said Liz. 'My aunts are all pretty old and boring.'

'She's great,' Emma agreed. Yes, with Aunt Ed there, she knew she had one person at home who wasn't going to treat her like a baby!

4

Being hugged by Aunt Ed was an unforgettable experience. Like her brother, Emma's father, Aunt Ed was tall and well-built and very strong. When she eventually let go, Emma felt quite breathless – and she had bits of fluff from Aunt Ed's sweater tickling her nose. 'It's lovely to see you!' Aunt Ed exclaimed.

Seeing Aunt Ed here in the sitting-room made Emma want to laugh. Everything in the room was dull and old-fashioned, but Aunt Ed was the total opposite. She wore a brilliant pink sweater with a red and green parrot on the front, and earrings with little parrots on them too. Her lips were bright pink and her hair was blond, because she dyed it – as she'd cheerfully admitted to Emma's mum on her last visit. Mrs Pennington had been a bit disapproving. She refused to cover up the grey hairs that were beginning to appear. She said they were natural. 'Blow nature,' Aunt Ed had retorted, 'I'm not going to be an old fogey.' That had upset Mrs Pennington.

'I'm not an old fogey!' she'd protested when Aunt Ed had gone. But looking at the two together now, Emma wasn't so sure. Her mum looked nice in her green and white dress, but she didn't look very exciting. But Aunt Ed was like an exotic bird. No one could call *her* an old fogey!

'Are you going to sit down and have some tea?' asked Aunt Ed, pointing to the tray on the coffee table. 'Your mum's made a wonderful chocolate cake. I've had three slices already!'

'I'll be back in a minute,' Emma said, nodding. 'I want to hear all about your journey, but I've got something to do first.' All the way home from school she'd been wondering how she was going to wash her borrowed gym kit without her mother knowing about it. This was the perfect opportunity. Emma could put them in the washing machine while her mum and Aunt Ed were chatting.

She left her school bag on the kitchen table and went out to the laundry room. Her mum hadn't emptied the last wash out of the machine, and Emma had to get the laundry basket and tumble all the damp shirts and pillow cases into it. Then she threw the joggers and the T-shirt in.

'Washing liquid,' she muttered to herself, looking round for the bottle. Where had her mother hidden it? She was so busy opening the cupboards and searching, she didn't hear footsteps behind her.

'What's the problem, love?' Mrs Pennington stood there, holding the teapot in one hand.

'I just wanted to wash a couple of things, that's all.' Emma knew that she must look guilty. She'd never been very good at hiding her feelings.

'Why don't you just put them in the laundry basket with all the other washing?'

'Because . . . I need to do them quickly for school tomorrow.' It was the best excuse she could think of.

'What do you need for school?' Mrs Pennington became suspicious. She bent down and reached into the machine. 'What are these?' She pulled out the joggers and top.

Emma screwed up her face in despair. Was there nothing she could keep a secret from her parents? Did they have to know about everything she did? 'They're just some gym kit that the gym teacher gave me to wash. I've got to take them back in case some-one else needs them.' Emma tried to make it sound casual, but her mother wasn't so easily put off.

'But why are you washing someone else's gym kit?' she asked.

'It's not someone else's.' Emma stared at her feet, feeling awkward. 'It's spare kit. The new gym teacher gave it to me to wear this afternoon.'

'But you don't do gym,' said her mother, confused.

'She wanted me to try playing volleyball, so she lent me the clothes.'

Mrs Pennington looked shocked. 'But we wrote to the school and explained that you weren't to do gym or games because of the danger of hurting yourself.' She walked back into the kitchen, Emma trailing miserably behind. 'Have they been forcing you to do gym?'

'No, Mum. It was just today – and I really enjoyed it. I'm good at it!' Emma exclaimed.

The large pink figure of Aunt Ed appeared in the kitchen doorway. 'What's this you're good at?' she asked cheerfully.

'I was telling Mum I've been playing volleyball,' Emma explained. 'It was my first game—'

'And your last,' Mrs Pennington said flatly, turning on the kettle and reaching for the teabags. 'Honestly, Edna, can you believe it? When Emma started at Bell

Street we made it clear that she wasn't allowed to take part in sports in case she hurt herself. Last week she came home and announced that she wanted to go rock climbing and canoeing with the school and now they've got her playing volleyball!'

'If she enjoys it, what's the problem?' Aunt Ed shrugged.

'I do like it,' Emma said plaintively.

'That's not the point.' Mrs Pennington poured boiling water into the teapot with a sigh. 'They shouldn't be encouraging Emma to do these things. It's irresponsible – and it upsets her when we have to clamp down on them.'

Aunt Ed looked as if she wanted to say something, but she just pursed her lips and kept quiet.

'Mum, please, I'm fine,' begged Emma. 'I didn't even fall over. It was great – we beat Gina Galloway's team and she was furious!'

Mrs Pennington shook her head slowly and turned her back. 'I'm glad you had a good time, Emma, but it would be best if you don't do it again.'

'But Mum, you're being totally unfair!' Emma snapped. When her mother turned her back like that and ignored her, it made her more angry than ever. Mrs Pennington looked amazed at her outburst.

'I don't know what's come over you, Emma. Shouting like this, when we have a guest.' Her mother stared at her icily, but Emma didn't care. Aunt Ed would understand, she knew. 'If you keep going on about it, your father and I may decide that you're not mature enough to go to the school disco.'

Emma was silent – and furious, too. Mrs Pennington cast a glance at Aunt Ed, standing in the doorway and then added, 'You've got to understand that we have to be tough with you for your own sake, Emma. One day, when you're older, you'll see that it makes sense.'

Aunt Ed coughed. It was an ordinary enough cough, but there was something about it that suggested that Aunt Ed didn't agree. Her lips were pressed in a thin pink line, as if she'd shut them tight in case the wrong words popped out. She raised one eyebrow questioningly.

There was a long, tense silence, broken only by the ticking of the clock. Emma felt tears of frustration pricking her eyelids, but she held them back. Her parents might treat her like a baby, but she wasn't going to act like one.

Finally Aunt Ed sighed. 'Why don't we go and have a slice of that cake? I find there's nothing like chocolate cake for making everyone feel better.' As she turned in the doorway, she looked at Emma with a sympathetic expression.

Emma managed a little smile in return. Somehow she felt confident that Aunt Ed understood her problem. But what could an aunt from Australia do, when her parents were so determined to protect her?

'Emma and I will do the washing-up,' Aunt Ed announced after supper that evening.

'Thanks, Aunt Ed.' Andrew grinned at Emma – it was his turn to do the dishes this evening.

'You should go and rest,' suggested Mr Pennington. 'You must be jet-lagged after your flight.'

Aunt Ed gave Emma the merest hint of a wink. 'Oh, I think we can manage the dishes – unless you're scared I'll break a plate or two?'

'Of course not,' murmured Mrs Pennington.

'Then that's settled.' Aunt Ed began to gather the dishes. 'The rest of you can go and watch television or study your law books,' she said brightly, nodding at Mr Pennington. 'Emma and I can have a good chat while we work.' She reached out and gave Emma a one-armed hug. 'I want a chance to get to know you again. You've grown up so much since I was last here.'

'It's very kind of you, Edna,' Mrs Pennington said. 'If you want to do the washing-up, I know it's no use arguing with you.' There was a slight edge in her voice.

'Alone at last,' said Aunt Ed when they'd gone. She shut the door quietly. 'Now we can have a good gossip. What have you been up to recently? Any adventures?' She smiled mischievously.

When Aunt Ed was like this, Emma found it difficult to believe that she was more than fifty years old. She was just like a big kid! It was so easy to talk to her – not like other adults.

'I wish I *could* have some adventures,' Emma said ruefully as she dried off the glasses. 'But you saw what happened this afternoon. I'm not even allowed to play volleyball.'

'And what was this about rock climbing?' Aunt Ed asked, looking puzzled. 'Where are you off to? Mount Everest?'

Emma giggled. 'No, only to Wales. Except I'm not allowed to go.' She told her all about the adventure weekend and the argument over it.

Aunt Ed shrugged when she'd finished. 'It sounds

great. I wish they'd done that sort of thing when I was at school.'

'I think it sounds great, you think it sounds great – and Mum and Dad think it sounds terrible.'

'I guess they worry about you a lot,' murmured Aunt Ed.

'I know they do,' Emma sighed. 'The problem is, I don't think they're ever going to let me grow up and do the kind of things everyone else takes for granted.'

Aunt Ed rinsed off a plate. 'It's difficult for them, I can see that. You're their youngest child – the baby of the family. They don't want to see you grow up and leave the nest like your sisters.'

'But they've got to let me go,' Emma said indignantly. 'They've got to stop treating me like a baby and realise that I'm twelve years old!'

'Twelve?' Aunt Ed smiled. 'That old already, eh? You know,' she added thoughtfully, 'I can remember when you were born. Your mum and dad were very proud of you, of course, but they were desperately worried about your leg. They thought that in some way it was their fault. All they wanted for you was to be able to walk properly.'

Aunt Ed stared out of the window into the garden, where Oscar the cat was lazing under a bush. 'Each time you went into hospital for an operation, they used to worry in case it wasn't a success. And they hated seeing you in pain or wearing a plaster cast. So you see it's understandable, now you *can* walk and run, that they're terrified something will happen and put you back where you started.'

Emma slowly dried a plate, taking in what Aunt

46

Ed had said. She'd never thought about how much her parents must have suffered while she was in hospital. 'I can understand all that,' she said softly. 'But even so, it's still difficult for me.'

'I know.' Aunt Ed held out her soapy hands and blew the bubbles into the air. 'Overprotecting a child is almost as bad as not taking enough care of it. Everyone needs a chance to develop some independence.'

'Exactly,' agreed Emma. 'But what can I do to get Mum and Dad to see that?'

Aunt Ed shook her head until her parrot earrings swung. 'I'm not sure,' she said. 'All you can really do is keep chipping away at them and hope that one day they'll see that for your own good you need to take a few risks. After all, that's what makes life worth living.'

'I sometimes wonder if they're right,' Emma mused. 'Maybe the things I want to do are too dangerous.'

Aunt Ed put her head on one side. 'Well, if everyone keeps telling you everything is dangerous it's natural for you to believe them. But you're a sensible girl, Emma. I'm sure you know what's safe and what's not. You have to trust your own instincts when it comes to these things. If you really think you can play volleyball or manage the activities on the adventure weekend, I reckon you're probably right.'

'Yes, I reckon I am,' Emma nodded, feeling suddenly much more confident. Aunt Ed had summed up pretty much what she had been feeling.

Aunt Ed grinned and stuck out her chin. 'And I've always found that the only way to get what I've wanted from life is to go for it full out.'

But how was Emma going to get her parents to change their minds? She'd tried persuading them and it didn't work. It would take forever for them to see that she had to be allowed to do the things everyone else did. If she was going to make them see she was growing up, she'd have to do something really dramatic – and she'd have to do it soon!

'Andrew, I need that pound you owe me.' Emma stuck her head round her brother's bedroom door. He was supposed to be doing his homework but instead he was jerking his head from side to side in time to the music playing on his personal stereo. Emma laughed, he looked so silly.

'What do you want?' He switched the stereo off once he saw her laughing at him.

'I've come for that pound you borrowed last week,' Emma repeated.

'Do you really need it? I'm short of cash now. I'll let you have it next week.'

'I need it right now.' Emma was determined. 'Next week will be too late.'

Andrew got up with a groan and opened a drawer. He kept his back turned to her, in case she saw where he kept his secret hoard of small change. 'Here you are. It's practically every penny I've got,' he said, giving her a pile of coins.

'Hard luck.' She didn't feel sorry for him. He was always wasting his allowance on comics and junk and then borrowing money from her.

'What are you going to spend it on?' he asked, scratching his top lip where his moustache was still failing to grow properly.

Emma stuck her chin in the air. 'That's my business,' she said, looking mysterious. Let him think what he liked!

Back in her room she dropped the coins into the tin where she kept all her cash and began to add everything up. With what she had here and the money in her savings account, maybe, just maybe, she'd have enough.

But no. However many times she added the figures up, and however many times she double-checked the price printed on the handout, she still didn't have enough to cover the cost of the adventure weekend. She was nearly fourteen pounds short – and where was she going to find fourteen pounds in a hurry? Miss Tyler was warning people that they had to bring in their signed forms and money by the end of the week.

And the form was another problem. Her parents would never sign it for her. Emma picked up her pen and tried writing her mother's name, Marjorie Pennington, on some scrap paper. But that was no good, either. If she wrote it using her right hand, it looked as if it was just her usual handwriting – and Miss Tyler would spot the forgery at once. If she wrote with her left hand, it looked as if a spider with muddy feet had run across the page. Miss Tyler wouldn't be fooled by that, either.

Emma sat and stared at the coins on the desk. It was horrible, but she'd better face up to the truth: there was no way she was going to go on the adventure weekend. Downstairs, doing the washing-up with Aunt Ed, it had seemed the answer to all her problems. She'd sign up and somehow fix it to go away with the rest of the class. How she'd manage to get away, she had no idea. But if she couldn't even book her place on the trip, the plan wasn't going to get off the ground. She couldn't go – and that was that.

She bit her lip hard. It felt as if her one and only chance to make a stand against her parents had disappeared like a balloon bursting. But the piles of coins on the table set her thinking. Maybe she couldn't afford to go on the adventure weekend, but with the money she had she *could* buy herself some new clothes. She'd go out tomorrow and get a copy of the magazine Liz and Jas had been looking at that morning. That would give her some ideas.

And if she was going to buy new clothes, why didn't she get something for the school disco? Something glamorous. She didn't have a thing she could wear to a disco. In fact she hardly had a thing she really liked wearing. Emma opened her wardrobe door and began to pull out the hangers, until the chair and bed and most of the floor was covered with garments.

It was a pretty depressing sight. Apart from two little-girlish dresses in flower-patterned cotton, Emma's clothes consisted mainly of baggy jeans and boring skirts in sensible colours. They all hung loosely around her hips because her mum had advised her that that way they didn't draw attention to her limp. To go with her skirts and trousers she had a collection of equally plain and sensible tops. There were no leggings, no mini-skirts, no brightly-coloured silky tops like the one Jas had pointed out in the magazine.

Emma stared at the clothes frostily. They'd have to go. She felt like packing them all up now and putting them in the bin. Was it any wonder she felt different from all the other girls if she *looked* so different too? Becky and Jas wouldn't be seen dead in any of her outfits!

Well, things were going to change. Early on Saturday morning she'd go into Wetherton shopping centre and buy herself the kind of clothes everyone else at school wore. She'd get some tights, too, like Liz's. And maybe she'd get a slide like Becky's for her hair. And lip gloss and eye-shadow. Her parents might not want her to do grown-up things, but they couldn't stop her looking like an ordinary twelve-year-old, could they?

5

'Have you finished with that screwdriver?' Charlie Farrel asked. The class were spending the morning in the workshop, putting together their design projects.

'Nearly.' Emma gave the screw she was inserting one last turn. 'I think that's tight enough,' she said. 'What do you think?'

Charlie peered through her glasses and twiddled a strand of red hair as she looked at the object Emma was holding out. 'What exactly is it?'

'It's a nesting-box!' Emma exclaimed. 'Can't you see? The hole here is for the bird to go through.'

'It's not very big,' Charlie commented.

'It's for small birds – like sparrows and blackbirds.' Emma raised her eyebrows. 'What did you think it was going to be for? An eagle?'

'Very funny,' said Charlie, straight-faced. 'Will a blackbird be able to get through there?' She didn't seem convinced.

'That's what it says on the worksheet.' Emma pointed to the diagram she'd been following. 'Maybe it's for thin blackbirds.'

They both laughed. 'Well, at least yours is going better than my project,' Charlie sighed. 'This is supposed to be a box to keep my bangles in, but I can't get the lid to fit. Miss Tyler's just told me to take the hinges off and try again for the fourth time.'

'Here's the screwdriver.' Emma handed it over and Charlie put her box down on the bench and began dismantling it. 'What's wrong with Liz? She's been looking really upset.'

Charlie pushed up the sleeves of the baggy navy shirt she was wearing and glanced over to the bench where Liz was sawing pieces of timber. 'She's down because she doesn't think she can go on the adventure weekend.'

'Why not?' Emma asked, feeling curious. 'Won't her parents let her go?' Maybe she wasn't the only one whose parents were worried about the dangers of rock climbing and horse riding.

'Ouch!' Charlie sucked her thumb, where she'd stabbed it with the screwdriver. 'No, her parents don't mind her going, they just say it's too expensive. Unless she can get them to change their minds she won't be able to go.'

'That's too bad.' Emma knew how disappointed Liz must feel. She'd been feeling pretty down herself in the last few days, despite Aunt Ed's attempts to cheer her up.

From across the workshop came the sound of someone playing a tune on an electronic keyboard. 'Hey,' said Charlie, looking up, 'Jamie must have got his keyboard working!' Emma looked puzzled. She tried not to pay too much attention to anything Jamie did, in case he thought she was showing an interest in him.

'Haven't you seen it?' asked Charlie. 'He's making a proper keyboard. He bought the microchip and built the circuits himself. He's really clever, you know.'

'Is he?' Emma commented vaguely, deliberately trying to avoid the subject of Jamie Thompson. He was really good at Technology, though, she had to admit. 'Poor Liz,' she said, changing the subject.

'Yeah,' agreed Charlie, dropping a screw on the floor and bending to pick it up. 'So she probably won't be coming to Wales with the rest of us. How about you?'

Emma wrinkled her nose. 'I'd really like to come, but my parents are being a bit funny about it.'

'Maybe they'll change their minds,' suggested Charlie.

'Maybe.' But Emma didn't hold out much hope. To be honest, she'd given up all thoughts of going on the adventure weekend. It was an impossible dream. 'I need to go and get some sandpaper,' she decided. Leaving her nesting-box on the bench, she went to the cupboard. The sandpaper was kept on the bottom shelf, so Emma had to kneel down on the floor to look for it. Down there she was almost hidden from view behind the cupboard door.

'Hi, Charlie.' It was Gina Galloway's posh voice she could hear. 'I'm next for that screwdriver you're using. I heard you say Liz may not be able to go on the adventure weekend. How about you?'

'Sure, I'm going,' Emma heard Charlie say. 'And Jas and Becky have already handed in their forms. Emma's coming too, if she can get her parents to agree to it.'

Gina sniffed loudly. Emma could just imagine the sneering look on her face. 'Let's hope they say no,'

Gina continued. 'If she does come we'll have to spend all our time looking after her.'

'What do you mean?' Charlie sounded surprised.

'Well, it's not supposed to be a holiday for the disabled, is it?' said Gina. Hidden behind the cupboard door, Emma could feel her ears burning.

'She's not disabled,' Charlie snapped. 'She beat you at volleyball the other day, didn't she?'

'Volleyball's one thing, but canoeing and rock climbing are something else,' Gina said flatly. 'She'll be too scared to do anything and we'll have to spend all our time babysitting her.'

'That's a mean thing to say.' Charlie sounded angry.

Gina made a bored sort of yawning sound. 'It's not just her disability, is it? She's such a goody-goody. If she comes to Wales, we won't be able to relax and have fun.'

That was too much for Emma. She jumped up furiously from behind the cupboard door. 'Why don't you say that to my face, Gina, instead of making your nasty remarks behind my back?'

Gina gave a sickly smile that didn't reach her cold grey eyes. 'Emma! Were you hiding?' She wagged a finger at Emma, whose fists were curled up in balls of rage. 'You know what they say – eavesdroppers never hear anything nice about themselves.'

'*You* never say anything nice about anyone!' Emma tried to keep her voice down so that Miss Tyler didn't hear, but it was difficult, she was so angry. 'Why don't you just shut up and go away? We don't want to listen to your nonsense.'

'Yeah,' said Charlie, nodding firmly. 'Just leave us alone.'

Gina was white with fury. She stomped off across the workshop, her hair bobbing up and down with each angry step.

'Whew!' Charlie whistled through her teeth. 'You showed her! I've never seen you so furious before, Emma.'

'Well I've had enough of her.' Emma grabbed the nesting-box and began to sand it down with a vengeance. 'Who does she think she is?'

'Well, from now on you'd better be careful. If I know Gina, now you've stood up to her she'll really try and put you down,' Charlie warned.

'Let her try,' snarled Emma. 'There's nothing she can say that will hurt me.' But then a terrible thought struck her.

What if there had been some truth in what Gina had said about her going on the adventure holiday? What if Gina wasn't the only one in the class who thought Emma needed looking after? What if they all thought she was no fun? It made her feel sick to think of what they might be saying behind her back.

There had to be a way of proving them wrong and showing them that she was perfectly capable of standing on her own two feet. But what was she going to do?

When Emma walked into the living room after school, she found Aunt Ed dozing on the sofa, snoring away with her mouth open and her feet propped up on a cushion. Oscar was lying on her lap. As Emma walked in, he leapt up and his tail brushed Aunt Ed's nose.

'What's that? Eh?' Aunt Ed opened her eyes in

mid-snore. 'Oooh!' She sat up slowly. 'This sofa isn't very comfortable, is it? I'm stuck!'

Emma went to the rescue, offering a hand to pull Aunt Ed upright. Today her aunt was wearing bright pink trousers and a purple blouse. She had matching purple sandals and her toenails were painted pink to go with the trousers.

'Thank you, darling,' Aunt Ed said with a smile, once she was properly awake. 'I was just having a quick snooze. I've been out shopping most of the day and it's exhausting. Did you have a good day at school?'

'Not exactly,' Emma admitted. She perched on the arm of the sofa.

'Want to tell me about it?' asked Aunt Ed, checking that her parrot earrings were still in place.

'It's nothing new,' Emma said with a sigh. 'It's just that everyone's going on the adventure weekend except me and Liz Newman. And Gina Galloway's telling everyone how glad she is I'm not going.' Emma told her the full story.

'That Gina sounds like a spoiled brat,' Aunt Ed said firmly when Emma had finished.

'She is!' Emma giggled. 'Her parents give her anything she wants. I just wish I could go to Wales to prove her wrong. I'd like to push her off a cliff.'

Aunt Ed laughed, then shook her head sadly. 'It's a pity your parents are so determined not to let you go. You know, all this reminds me of the time *my* parents banned me from going to a New Year's dance in our home town. They said I wasn't old enough, even though I was seventeen.'

'Seventeen?' Emma gasped. 'But that's – ancient!'

Aunt Ed's eyes twinkled. 'I suppose it must seem ancient to you! My parents wanted me to stay home and celebrate the New Year with them, not with strangers, you see.'

'So what did you do?'

'I climbed out of my bedroom window in my lovely dress, and went to the dance anyway. They'd threatened me with all kinds of punishments if I disobeyed them – but it didn't stop me!' Aunt Ed smiled wickedly.

'What happened?' asked Emma, wide-eyed.

'All hell broke loose when I got back home.' Aunt Ed closed her eyes, remembering it. 'My father shouted, my mother wouldn't speak to me. I was locked in my room for hours on end. What a scene! They stopped my allowance and grounded me for a month, I remember. But it blew over before long.' She smiled again at Emma, her eyes twinkling with the memory. 'And you know what?'

'No,' Emma prompted.

'I didn't regret it one bit!' Aunt Ed threw back her head and laughed loudly. 'It was worth all the trouble because at that dance I met your Uncle Robert. We got married just a few years later and were so happy together.' Aunt Ed looked wistful. Emma had never met Uncle Robert. He had died in Australia when she was very young. She and Aunt Ed sat sadly together for a moment.

'So you see,' said Aunt Ed, 'sometimes it pays to be rebellious. Sometimes when you're young, you have to do what's best for you, even though your parents can't understand.'

'Were they very strict with you?' Emma plumped

up a cushion and settled down next to Aunt Ed on the sofa.

'Oh yes, very old-fashioned. I was the oldest, so I was the one to break all the rules first. But I wasn't the only one to disobey them, you know.'

There were footsteps in the hall and Emma's father walked in. He was wearing a smart suit, but even when he was all dressed up, he still had a teddy-bearish look about him. 'What's this you're telling Emma, Ed?' he asked cheerfully, giving them both a kiss.

Aunt Ed glanced conspiratorially at Emma. 'We were talking about when I was a girl,' she said with an air of complete innocence.

Mr Pennington shook his head as he dropped into one of the armchairs. 'There must be hundreds of stories to tell because you were always getting into trouble. Do you remember the time you tipped a plate of stew over my head? And when you got stuck up that apple tree in our neighbours' garden and had to be rescued?'

Aunt Ed roared with laughter. 'I'd forgotten about the stew. You were being such a horrible little brother, so I just picked up my plate and put it on your head. You did look funny!'

'You never told me about that, Dad!' Emma giggled, grabbing his arm.

Mr Pennington was laughing so much his eyes were watering. He put his arm round her shoulder. 'I can remember sitting there with carrots and pota- toes dripping down my neck. It took our mother ages to get the gravy out of my hair! I had the naughtiest big sister in the world.'

Aunt Ed held up her finger. 'Now don't pretend

you were perfect, Phil. You got into trouble a few times yourself,' she reminded him.

'No!' Mr Pennington protested, but his twinkling eyes gave him away.

'Oh, yes you did!' Aunt Ed tut-tutted. 'What a bad memory you've got. Have you forgotten the time you sneaked off school to go fishing and fell in the river?'

'No, he hasn't,' said Emma, 'because he's told me about it.'

'And I don't believe you've forgotten your adventure in London,' added Aunt Ed. She said 'London' very emphatically, as if it had a secret meaning. 'You can't deny that you were a tearaway.'

'What happened in London?' Emma pinched her father's chin. 'Come on, let's hear all about it.'

'Nothing happened,' Mr Pennington insisted. 'Everyone made a huge fuss about nothing. I was only young. It was the kind of mistake anyone might make.'

Aunt Ed roared with laughter and Emma's dad began to giggle. 'You've got to tell me!' Emma groaned. 'What happened in London?'

Mr Pennington shook his head. 'I think it's best left forgotten!'

Just then the phone rang. Mr Pennington got up, still pink-cheeked from all the laughing.

'Saved by the bell,' he gasped, as he went off to his study to answer the call.

Aunt Ed watched him go, then faced Emma. She seemed amused. 'Perhaps I'd better not tell you about his adventures in London if he doesn't want me to. But I can promise you, your father wasn't always as starchy and serious as he seems now.'

For a moment Aunt Ed looked a little wistful. 'You know, to me he'll always be my naughty little brother – even if he has turned into a sensible grown-up, bossing his own children around.'

'He may be grown up, but he won't let me do it,' Emma grumbled. 'He and Mum want to keep me like a little girl.'

'Being a grown-up isn't so wonderful,' snorted Aunt Ed. 'There's nothing wrong with being young. People keep telling me I should act my age – but I don't want to get too sensible and serious.'

Emma looked at her aunt, with her pink toenails and purple top and her crazy ideas. She tried to imagine her in a neat beige skirt and matching blouse, with grey hair – and without a pair of parrot earrings in sight. The thought made her shiver. 'Please, Aunt Ed,' she said seriously. 'Promise me that you'll never grow up!'

6

Emma was up early on Saturday. There were so many things to pack into the day, she needed an early start. She'd just finished her toast and was halfway up the stairs on her way to brush her teeth, when Aunt Ed appeared on the landing. She wore a red satin kimono with golden dragons embroidered on the sleeves and back. Emma had never seen anything like it before. Aunt Ed looked like a character from a glitzy soap opera!

'Are you going into town?' Aunt Ed asked.

'Yes, I want to get to the shopping centre the minute it opens,' Emma said. She already knew exactly which shops she wanted to visit.

Aunt Ed turned and went back towards her bedroom. 'Perhaps I can ask you a favour, dear.' Emma followed her. Aunt Ed's room smelled lovely, just like the perfume she always wore. If Emma had enough money left after she'd bought herself some clothes, maybe she'd buy a bottle of perfume, too.

She noticed Aunt Ed's suitcase in the corner. It had a big label on it with 'Edna Gibson' written in a flowery, distinctive style, and there was a little circle over the i. Even Aunt Ed's handwriting was out of the ordinary!

'Would you post this for me?' asked Aunt Ed, handing her a letter. 'I'll give you the money for the stamp.' She opened her purse. Emma noticed that the letter was for Aunt Ed's daughter in Australia. 'Send it air mail, won't you,' Aunt Ed said with a gleam in her eye. 'The quicker it gets there, the quicker we'll have the reply.'

'No problem,' said Emma. 'I'll see you at lunchtime.' She turned to leave. 'Don't forget we're going to the school fête. I'm helping on our class's stall.'

'I'll be ready,' promised Aunt Ed. 'Hold on a second, though.' She opened her wallet. 'I didn't bring you a gift from Australia, Emma, because it's so long since I saw you I couldn't imagine what you'd like. I've been meaning to get you something, but I haven't found the right thing. So why don't you take this and get yourself something that you want?' She held out twenty-five pounds.

'Thank you!' Emma gasped with surprise. It was the most money she'd ever been given in her life.

Aunt Ed patted her shoulder. 'You're welcome, my dear. You deserve something special and you know what you really want far better than I do.'

'I'll buy something extra special,' Emma assured her. She was so excited, it was difficult to breathe. And was she imagining it, or did Aunt Ed really give her a big wink?

Emma emerged from the Post Office deep in thought. When she'd got up this morning she'd known exactly what she was going to do today. But suddenly she had an unexpected decision to make. Aunt Ed's gift meant that she had enough money to go on the adventure weekend if she wanted to – and if it wasn't already too late. Or she could spend it on a really great outfit for the disco. Which was it going to be?

Something else bothered her, too. What did Aunt Ed's wink mean? After what she'd said yesterday about young people sometimes having to rebel against their parents, was Aunt Ed encouraging her to go to Wales? Emma was perplexed.

If she chose the adventure weekend, Emma still had to work out how she was going to get away from home. And then there was the problem of getting a signature on the consent form. As she crossed the road to the shopping mall, Emma had a horrible thought: what if she handed over all the money for the adventure weekend and then couldn't get away for the weekend after all? She'd lose everything. That was something she hadn't thought of before.

She still hadn't made up her mind what to do when she arrived at the top of the escalator in the shopping centre. Ahead of her was the first shop she'd planned to try, a boutique called Matt.

Emma hesitated. The clothes in the window seemed so trendy in comparison to the jeans and plain white T-shirt she was wearing. For a minute she was tempted to go off to one of the boring old chain stores where her mother always bought her clothes. But just then a top in the window caught her eye. It was a peach colour and made out of silky-looking material, just like the top Jas had pointed out in the fashion magazine the other day. And with it, the model in the window was wearing a pair of velvety black leggings. Emma braced herself, held her chin high and walked straight into the shop.

Five minutes later she stepped gingerly out of the changing cubicle to have a look at herself in the fitting-room mirror. There was no one else around, thank goodness, so Emma was able to twirl in front of the mirror without other people staring. The peach-coloured top looked good. It had a V-shaped neck and was fastened with a row of tiny pearl buttons. It was the nicest thing Emma had ever worn. And she loved the smooth black leggings, too.

Emma stood back and stared. It was difficult to believe it was her in the mirror. She hadn't realised she had such long legs. The colour of the top made her skin glow, too. She had half expected to look stupid, but instead she looked great – a new Emma, pretty and fashionable.

'What a transformation!' a voice behind her called out.

Emma swung round in alarm. Gina Galloway was standing watching, her arms piled with items she'd brought to try on. 'That's really nice,' Gina said. There was a nasty edge to her voice. 'I think I'll get a top like that for myself.'

Emma's heart fell with a thud. That would be awful – and that was probably why Gina had said it. She didn't really want the top for herself. She just wanted to ruin Emma's pleasure.

'It certainly makes a change from your usual gear, doesn't it? Do you think your mummy will like it?' Gina asked nastily.

'It's not up to my mum,' Emma said calmly.

'Well, if you get it, remember not to fall over, or you'll ruin the effect!' And with a giggle, Gina flounced into a changing cubicle and pulled the curtain.

Emma stood frozen to the spot for what seemed

like ages. She was amazed when she looked in the mirror that steam wasn't pouring out of her ears. Who did Gina Galloway think she was?

When Emma came out of the fitting-room, Gina was standing in front of the mirror admiring herself in a frilly green dress. Her hair was fluffed out like a blond poodle's. 'What do you think?' she asked.

'You look like a Brussels sprout,' Emma snapped, heading for the cash desk. She put the top back on the rail. If Gina was getting one, Emma didn't want it. But she took the leggings over to the assistant. 'I'll take these, please,' she said firmly. *Thanks, Gina Galloway*, Emma thought as she waited to pay. *You've helped me make up my mind.*

'What time are we going to the school fête?' asked Mrs Pennington. She was in the garden cutting flowers and her back was turned to Emma, who'd just got back from the shops.

'I need to help on our class stall at one o'clock,' Emma explained. 'You can come on later if you want.' She held back the branch of a rose bush that had snagged her mum's skirt.

'Oh, no, I'd like to be there when it starts. Otherwise I'll miss the best bargains!' She turned round with a big smile, then narrowed her eyes. 'There's something different about you. Is that lipstick you're wearing?'

'It's lip gloss,' Emma corrected. 'It stops my lips getting dry.'

Emma could almost hear her mum thinking about it for a few seconds before she said, 'It looks very nice. But you know, Emma, you're pretty enough not to need a lot of make-up.'

66

Emma blushed. Her mother had never told her she was pretty before. 'It's okay, Mum,' she said softly. 'I'm not going to start slapping it on with a trowel.'

Mrs Pennington smiled. 'That's good.' She handed Emma the bunch of roses she'd just cut – and it was then she noticed the leggings. 'And you've bought yourself some clothes, too!' She stepped back to take a look. Emma watched a frown descend over her forehead.

'Aren't they a bit tight, love?'

'That's how they're supposed to look,' Emma explained. 'I could have bought a much more clingy pair if I'd wanted.'

'I'm glad you didn't!' Mrs Pennington raised her eyebrows. 'I'm sorry, Emma, but I can't pretend I like them. They're very revealing. Couldn't you get yourself a proper pair of trousers?'

'But I wanted leggings, not trousers. Trousers aren't fashionable,' Emma persisted, feeling really disappointed. Why did her mum have to be such a fuddy-duddy?

Mrs Pennington raised her hand. 'Look, why don't we go shopping together next weekend? I was thinking just the other day that you needed a few more outfits. We could get you something nice – something a bit more practical than these.'

'But these *are* practical,' Emma argued. 'They're really comfortable and stretchy. All my friends at school are wearing them.'

'Why copy them?' asked Mrs Pennington with a shrug. 'Why not dress in your own style?'

Emma shook her head in exasperation. Why was

it so difficult to make her mother understand? 'I just want to be in fashion, like everyone else,' she explained. 'Weren't you ever interested in fashion?'

'Fashions come and go,' said Mrs Pennington, not answering the question properly. 'This month it's leggings, next month it'll be something else. Anyway, you're only twelve. You don't have to start thinking about clothes till you're older.'

Emma felt so exasperated she thought she'd burst. 'But at school the girls think about clothes all the time! I'm growing up, Mum! I'm not a child any more.'

Her mother picked up the flowers she'd put on the lawn. 'I think it's a mistake for you to want to grow up so fast,' she replied. 'Why do you have to be like all the other girls in your class? What's right for them isn't necessarily right for you.'

'But how can I know what's right for me unless I'm allowed to experiment a bit?' cried Emma. 'You don't even give me the chance to try new things out.'

Mrs Pennington put her hand to her head as if it was beginning to ache. 'I don't know what's happening, Emma. You never used to behave like this. Can't you just calm down and be a good girl?'

'No!' Emma stormed up the garden path to the kitchen door. 'I'm sick of being a good girl!'

'Miss Tyler, is it too late for me to reserve a place on the adventure weekend?' Emma stood at the teacher's desk with her hands behind her back and her fingers crossed.

Miss Tyler raised her eyebrows behind her huge

red-rimmed glasses. 'Well, it *should* be too late, but because of the fête and all the other things I've had to do recently, I haven't got around to finalising the arrangements. So you're in luck, Emma, if you want to come.' She smiled.

'Great!' Emma sighed with relief. 'Here's the money.' She handed over an envelope with the notes Aunt Ed had given her, plus the money she'd taken from her savings account.

'Oh, I didn't realise it would be cash.' Miss Tyler seemed surprised. 'I was expecting a cheque.'

'Oh.' Emma blushed. What a stupid mistake to make. Of course everyone else would have paid with cheques written by their parents. Why didn't she think of that?

'Do you have your consent form?' Miss Tyler looked straight into Emma's eyes. Was she suspicious? Emma pulled out the sheet of blue paper and laid it on the desk.

In the space for the signature the name *Edna Gibson* had been written in a large and sprawling hand. Miss Tyler adjusted her glasses. 'Emma, who is Edna Gibson? Why haven't your parents signed the form?' She seemed concerned.

Emma bit her bottom lip and tried not to show how anxious she was feeling. 'It's all right, Miss Tyler, they know all about the trip.' Well, that was true enough, wasn't it? 'That signature is my Aunt Ed from Australia. She's staying with us at the moment. She encouraged me to go on the trip and gave me the money towards it, so I asked her to sign the consent form.'

Miss Tyler nodded slowly. 'Yes, now I come to

69

think of it I met your aunt at the fête on Saturday. She mentioned how much you wanted to come on the trip. I'm glad you managed to organise it.'

Emma breathed a sigh of relief. For a minute there she'd thought Miss Tyler was going to ask too many awkward questions. Like why Aunt Ed's signature was so huge. Emma didn't want to confess that she'd traced it from the luggage label on her aunt's suitcase.

She walked back down the aisle to her desk, aware that Gina Galloway was staring at her with her mouth wide open in surprise. Good!

Jamie Thompson caught Emma's eye. 'I'm really glad you're coming with us,' he whispered.

'Thanks.' Emma gave him a grin. Let the others think what they liked, she didn't care any more. There was no going back now. She'd forged Aunt Ed's signature, defied her parents' wishes and lied to Miss Tyler. Her days as a goody-goody were well and truly over.

It all felt really exciting – and terrifying. Emma was booked on the trip to Wales, but now she had to work out how she was going to get away from her parents for the weekend. And so far, she didn't have a single idea.

'Having trouble with your history homework?' Charlie came and sat down beside Emma in the library. 'I can't answer questions three and seven, can you?'

'Mmm?' Emma looked at her vaguely. She'd been a million miles away.

'You were looking really worried. I thought maybe Happy Heyward's homework assignment was giving you trouble,' repeated Charlie. Happy Heyward was Mr Heyward, and he was famous for his difficult homework projects and his bad temper when people couldn't complete them properly.

Charlie flung her long red hair back over her shoulder and a strand whipped across Emma's face and caught her in the eye. 'Whoops! Sorry.'

'That's okay.' Emma blinked hard. 'It's not history that's getting me down. It's the adventure weekend.'

Charlie looked surprised. 'I thought you wanted to come on it.'

'I *do*,' Emma said firmly.

'Well, you are coming on it – so why are you looking as if someone just told you you can't?' asked Charlie.

Emma gritted her teeth. She didn't know what to do, but things were getting desperate. She had to share her secret with someone. 'Charlie, if I tell you something, do you promise not to tell anyone else?'

'Of course!' Charlie grinned. 'Come on, what's going on? You've been looking pretty miserable ever since you booked the adventure weekend. You're not scared about it, are you?'

'No.' Emma shook her head. 'It's not that. It's – well, my parents don't know I'm going. They didn't want me to do it. They say it's not safe for me.'

'Wow!' Charlie whistled through her teeth. 'You've got a lot of nerve, Emma. What'll they do if they find out?'

Emma grimaced. 'I don't want to even think about it.' If she *did* start thinking about it, she was liable to burst into tears.

Charlie doodled a picture on her notepad. 'That

71

must be why your Aunt Ed signed the consent form.'

'Yes,' Emma said, nodding. She wouldn't tell Charlie that even Aunt Ed didn't know of the deception.

'I think I see the problem,' Charlie murmured, chewing the end of her pencil. 'If they don't know you're going, what are you going to tell them when you disappear for the weekend?'

Emma raised her eyebrows. 'I don't know. When I booked the holiday I thought I'd be able to come up with a way round it. But I can't see the answer.' Her voice sounded desperate even to her own ears.

'How about running away? The coach sets off right after school. All you have to do is get on it. They won't know you're missing till you get halfway to Wales.' Charlie shrugged. 'See, it's easy. Until you get back and have to face the music. I wouldn't want to be in your shoes then.'

Emma shook her head. 'You know my parents. If I'm not home by teatime they'll have the police out looking for me. What will Miss Tyler say when the coach gets chased by a police car?'

'Something pretty rude, I expect,' said Charlie. 'Well, if that won't work, how about leaving them a note, telling them where you've gone and that you'll be back on Sunday?'

'I thought of that,' Emma nodded. 'But I can just imagine them getting in the car and driving to Wales. They'd drag me out of the activities in front of everyone and make a big fuss. Gina Galloway would love every minute of it.'

'She's such a creep,' said Charlie, plaiting strands of her hair. It was something she often did when she was thinking hard. 'Well, if it's any help you can always say I've invited you to stay with me. You could say I asked you over for the weekend.'

'That's an idea. Thanks.' Emma tried to sound more cheerful, but to be honest she couldn't see how Charlie's suggestion was going to be any use. Her parents had never allowed her to sleep over at her friends' houses before, and they probably weren't going to start doing it now.

She'd better face facts. Unless there was a miracle, there was no way she could go on that adventure weekend . . .

7

'That was Edna,' Mrs Pennington called as she hung up the phone in the kitchen. 'She's broken her ankle.'

'She's done what?' Mr Pennington's study door was open and he'd heard the news. He came out into the hall. So did Emma, who'd been reading in the sitting-room.

'What happened?' she asked. 'Is she going to be okay?'

'She's going to be fine,' Mrs Pennington assured them. 'Apparently she was out walking in the street and a boy on a skateboard knocked her over. She's broken her ankle and the doctors have put her in plaster up to her knee.' Mrs Pennington shook her head in disbelief. 'It would happen to Edna, of course.'

'Poor Aunt Ed.' Emma remembered spending months at a time with her leg in plaster. It was horrible.

'Has she made arrangements to come back from Scotland?' Mr Pennington asked.

Aunt Ed had left Wetherton nearly two weeks earlier and had been travelling round visiting friends and relatives. She was due back in the next few days. 'That's one of the reasons she called,' said

Mrs Pennington. 'She can't travel by train, and her friends can't bring her back in the car. She wants to know if we can go and collect her at the weekend. It has to be the weekend – her friends are going away on holiday themselves next week.'

Mr Pennington frowned. He had a pencil behind his ear and a piece of sticky tape stuck to the back of his hand. He'd obviously been hard at work in his study. 'But I can't go this weekend! I'm going to my legal conference in Manchester. I'll be away till Sunday.'

'In that case I'll have to go.' Now it was Mrs Pennington's turn to look worried. 'But who's going to look after Emma? It's a long journey. I'll have to stay overnight.'

Emma did her best to look bothered, though inside she could feel her heart skip a beat. She'd been praying for a miracle all week, and here it was. 'I'll be all right,' she said calmly. 'Andrew will be here to keep an eye on me.'

Mrs Pennington laughed. 'Is that supposed to reassure us? If I know Andrew, he'll probably take the opportunity to stay out late. We can't leave you here all on your own, Emma. You'll have to come with me. Although it's a very long journey – and I don't know whether Edna's friends will have room for us both overnight. Maybe we should book into a hotel . . . ' She waved her hands in annoyance. 'Oh, why does it have to be so complicated?'

'I've got an idea,' Emma broke in, trying to make it sound as if she wasn't terribly keen. 'Charlie Farrel asked me to go and stay over with her one weekend. Why don't I ask her if it would be all right?' It wasn't a true blue lie, was it? After all, Charlie really had offered!

'Well, it would solve the problem.' Mrs Pennington looked at Emma and then at her husband thoughtfully. 'I've met Mrs Farrel at school. I'm sure she'd look after you well. And I think you're old enough to stay away on your own.'

'It's a good idea,' nodded her father. 'If we know you're safe at the Farrels', we won't have to worry about you.'

Emma tried to suppress her excitement. She wanted to jump in the air for joy. Instead she just said, 'I'll have a word with Charlie and see if it's all right, shall I?'

'Yes,' Mrs Pennington agreed. 'If you could stay with Charlie from Friday evening until Sunday lunchtime that would give me plenty of time for the journey and allow for any delays.'

'Can't Charlie and I have Sunday lunch together?' Emma asked quickly. The school trip wasn't due back till the early evening on Sunday. There was no way she could be back by lunchtime.

For a moment her mother seemed suspicious. Then she said, 'Only if Charlie's mother doesn't mind. Be sure to be back for tea, though. Aunt Ed will want to see you.'

'Okay.' Emma nodded. It was going to be a close thing, but maybe she could find some excuse for being a little late. 'It'll be fun staying over,' she said with a smile.

'You don't mind?' Mrs Pennington looked concerned. 'If you'd rather not do it, we can make some other arrangement.'

Emma shook her head. 'Don't worry about me. I'm really going to enjoy my weekend away from home, Mum.'

More than you know! she thought to herself with a secret smile.

'Toothbrush and washing kit?' asked Mrs Pennington after breakfast on Friday morning.

'Yes,' answered Emma, patting her backpack.

'Pyjamas, underwear, hairbrush?'

'Yes, yes, yes!' Emma laughed. 'Honestly, Mum, I've got everything I'm going to need. If I've forgotten anything I'm sure I can borrow from Charlie or—' She bit her tongue. She'd been just about to add 'or one of the other girls'. That might have given the game away. Fortunately her mother was too concerned about other things to notice the slip.

'Now you will be all right, Emma, won't you?' Mrs Pennington looked very serious and for a moment Emma felt guilty about her deception. Everything would have been so much easier if her parents had agreed to let her go on the adventure weekend in the first place, instead of making her mislead them like this. But bad as she felt about it, Emma wasn't going to call the whole thing off now.

'I'll be fine, Mum, I promise. I'll spend the whole weekend with Charlie,' she said truthfully. Mrs Pennington smiled and gave her a hug.

'I can remember when your sisters first stayed away overnight. It's a sure sign that you're growing up.' Her mother looked sad.

Emma picked up her backpack. She couldn't really understand what all the fuss was about. The other girls at school seemed to stay over at their friends' houses without making a big event of it.

'Right, I'll just say goodbye to Dad.'

Mr Pennington was in his study getting the paperwork ready for his conference. He gave Emma a hug.

'Have a lovely weekend.'

'I will,' Emma promised. She was going to have the best weekend ever!

'Did you see the parcel the postman delivered for you?' Mrs Pennington called as Emma opened the front door.

'I'll open it when I get back,' Emma replied. 'Bye, Mum.' She almost ran down the garden path and out into the street. In a few hours' time she'd be on her way to Wales – and nothing was going to stop her!

'Bye-bye, Bell Street!' cried Jas, as the coach pulled out of the school driveway. 'See you on Sunday.'

Emma felt a thrill of excitement as they set off down the hill and out through the centre of Wetherton. She was going away for the first time on her own, and tomorrow morning there'd be horse riding and canoeing. After all the worries and guilt of the last couple of weeks, she could hardly believe it was really happening.

Charlie, who was sitting next to her, gave her a mischievous glance. 'Well, it looks like you've done it, Emma. A secret weekend away.'

'Shhh!' Emma held her finger up to her lips.

Charlie pulled a camera out of her bag. 'It's great the whole class could come, including you two,' she said, nodding at Liz and Emma.

Liz laughed. 'Do you realise that this trip is my

birthday present? My parents said they couldn't afford this weekend *and* a birthday present, so I had to choose one or the other.'

'And you chose us,' Jas said with a giggle. 'How sweet.'

'After this, I can't have any other trips.' Liz sighed, looking genuinely sad. 'So it had better be good.'

'It'll be brilliant, I promise,' said Charlie. 'And I'm going to take lots of pictures, starting right now. Crowd together, please!' They all shouted 'cheese' as she took the snap.

Becky, who was sitting in the seat in front, turned round. 'When we get to the adventure centre we've got to make sure we all get in the same dorm, okay? Don't let anyone split us up. Think how horrible it would be to have to share a room with Gina!'

Charlie and Jas made gagging sounds. 'You're right,' Emma said, grinning. It was strange. Nothing had been said, but she really felt as if she'd joined the gang. Maybe they'd adopted her, or maybe she'd just changed. Whatever had happened, instead of feeling like an outsider looking in on everybody else, Emma suddenly felt as if she belonged with the others. It was a good feeling.

She glanced across the aisle of the bus. Jamie Thompson was sitting on his own, holding a computer magazine. But Emma could see that he was staring blank-faced out of the window. He looked lonely. She suddenly felt sad. No so very long ago, it might have been her sitting on her own like that.

'Would you like a chocolate chip cookie or some peanuts?' Becky was passing round a box of food – and they weren't even out of Wetherton yet.

'Thanks!' Emma took a packet of cookies and helped herself, then impulsively leaned across the aisle and tapped Jamie on the shoulder. 'How about a biscuit?'

'Thanks.' The tense look on his face melted for a moment as he helped himself.

'Do you still wish you weren't coming with us?' Emma asked him. 'Would you rather be at home with your computer?'

Jamie shrugged. 'The weekend won't be so bad. I just wish I felt as if I was part of the class. It's all right for you – you've got so many friends. You've all been together since you were at junior school.'

Emma bit into a cookie. It wasn't quite as simple as that. 'Becky's new,' she pointed out. 'She's only been at Bell Street a few weeks, but she fits in.'

Jamie frowned. 'That's just it. I feel as if I don't fit in and I don't know what to do to change it.'

'I know. I used to feel the same way,' Emma said, nodding.

'So what changed?'

'I'm not sure, really. I suppose I just decided to join in with everyone else more. Not sit on the sidelines and feel left out.'

'Maybe,' said Jamie, but he didn't look convinced.

Emma thought back to that day in the gym and the game of volleyball. As soon as she'd joined in, she'd felt like one of the team. Maybe that was they key – just joining in with whatever was going on and not waiting to be asked.

She'd done it, and here she was with her group of friends. But she couldn't do it for Jamie. If he wanted to join the crowd, he'd have to break the ice and get to know people himself. Maybe something would happen over the weekend to help. Emma hoped so.

Becky yawned loudly. 'It's no use, I'll have to go back to bed. I'm exhausted – and it's only eight o'clock!'

'Smile!' Charlie grinned and snapped another photo.

Miss Tyler, who was looking very bright in a red tracksuit, overheard Becky. 'That'll teach you to sit up talking half the night!' she said, laughing. 'I kept coming into your dorm and telling you to go to sleep, didn't I?'

'We did try,' said Becky, 'but none of us felt tired then.'

It was true, Emma agreed. Whenever Miss Tyler had come in and told them to be quiet, they'd settled down in their bunkbeds to sleep. And then someone would think of something she simply had to tell the others and they'd started chatting again. There was just so much to talk about!

'I didn't realise they were going to make us get up so early,' Jas muttered grouchily, trailing behind. They'd all been woken up at six-thirty to go on an early morning nature trail. 'I bet we were up before all the animals.'

'We probably woke them up,' Emma said with a giggle. 'I bet all the birds and squirrels were fast asleep before we came crashing through the trees, looking for them. They've probably all gone back now for a lie-in.'

'Maybe we could do that?' Jas asked hopefully.

'No,' said Miss Tyler. 'You haven't come all this way to sleep.'

'Hold on, everyone, I've dropped my owl pellet!' Charlie stopped in the middle of the path and they all searched for it.

They'd collected lots of things in the woods and put them in the plastic bags the instructors had handed out. Emma had some interesting tree bark and a strange mushroom. Clinton Walsh had found a dead stag beetle and was going round showing it off to everyone and scaring them.

A little further up the path and the activity centre came into view. 'Let's hope breakfast's ready, anyway,' Liz said cheerfully. The centre was really nice. There was a big central building with a dining room where they'd eaten last night, and a meeting room, where they'd all met after supper to hear about the plans for the weekend. They slept in log cabins among the trees. Each cabin had two dormitories with six bunk beds in each, and bathrooms.

'Everybody back to your cabins to wash your hands and put away your specimens,' instructed Miss Tyler. 'Breakfast will be in ten minutes.' There was a scream as Clinton threatened to drop the stag beetle down someone's neck.

'Clinton!' bellowed Miss Tyler. 'Bring that beetle here. I'm going to give it a decent burial.'

Emma went with the rest of the gang back to their cabin. Mina Stevens, who was in the other dorm in the cabin, came with them. 'You're really lucky you don't have the Red Peril in with you,' she said enviously.

'Who's the Red Peril?' asked Becky.

'That's our nickname for Miss Tyler. And you know what?' added Mina.

'What?' asked Emma.

'She snores!' The girls laughed so much they could hardly make it back to the cabin.

Emma washed her hands and ran a brush through her hair. For an instant she wondered what her parents were doing – but only for an instant. Maybe, she thought to herself, she should be feeling really guilty about deceiving them like this. But the truth was, she was having such a good time that she didn't care. Whatever happened when she got home, Emma didn't regret it one bit!

8

'Everybody out!'

Graham, the activities instructor, opened the door of the mini-bus and Emma and the rest of the group scrambled out into the sunshine in the stable yard. As she jumped down she caught her foot and landed clumsily on the gravel. Gina Galloway gave her a long-suffering glance, as if to say, 'Told you so.'

'Gather round,' commanded Graham, who was tall and dark and really cute-looking. 'Is everyone in the group here?'

'I'm here, Graham,' simpered Gina, fluttering her pale eyelashes at him. It made Emma feel sick, the way Gina was behaving. She was such a show-off. Everyone else was wearing jeans and ordinary shoes to go riding in, but Gina had brought her own jodhpurs, boots and riding hat. She looked as if she was ready for the Horse of the Year show.

Emma looked around the stables. There were girls mucking out ponies and horses waiting in the yard to be groomed. Beyond the buildings beautiful green hills rose up and in the distance Emma could see the mountains. This afternoon they'd probably be going there for rock climbing and abseiling.

Only one thing prevented it from being absolutely perfect. Emma just wished Liz and Becky and the others from her dorm were here in her group. It had been bad luck that when they'd been divided up for each of the activities, Emma had been standing in the wrong place. Right now, the others were canoeing in the river near the activity centre, while she was having to spend the whole day with Gina Galloway breathing down her neck. At least Jamie was here. He gave her his usual shy grin when she caught his eye. Emma blushed.

It was silly, but she was beginning to really like him. He wasn't like the other boys in the class, who were always playing jokes and getting into trouble. Before, Emma had felt a bit sorry for Jamie, but the more she got to know him, the more she felt friendly towards him. More than friendly, in fact.

Graham interrupted her thoughts. 'We're going on a two-hour pony trek,' he explained. 'First we'll get you equipped with crash hats, in case anyone falls off . . . '

Gina nudged Emma. 'We'd better get you an extra-safe one, hadn't we?' she whispered, just loud enough for Emma to hear. Emma nudged her back, hard.

'Ow!' Gina squeaked. Graham turned towards them.

'Behave yourselves, girls.' Emma went red. She couldn't seem to do anything even vaguely naughty without being told off.

Graham continued talking. 'When you've got your hats, we'll go and choose our ponies.'

'Perhaps they'll have a really old, quiet one for you,' muttered Gina. Emma felt like poking her really hard – but Graham was looking at them and she didn't dare.

It took only a few minutes for everyone to be fitted with a crash hat. 'I feel really silly,' complained Jamie, trying to brush his dark fringe out of his eyes.

'You look okay,' Emma reassured him, knocking on his hat with her knuckles. 'Rock solid,' she commented.

'Just like Gina's head – without a crash hat!' said Jamie, pulling a face. They walked out into the paddock. Tied up along a rail were eight ponies and three larger horses for the adults who were accompanying them on the trek.

'Choose your pony,' instructed Graham.

Emma walked along the rail, looking at them. It was difficult to know which to choose. Mina Stevens went up to a grey one and began stroking its nose. 'This one will do for me,' she said.

In the middle of the line was a chestnut pony with bright brown eyes. He tossed his head up and down with an alert look. Emma stopped by his side and he shook his head until his bridle jangled. He was lovely, but was he too lively for her? Emma watched him stamp his hoof. She'd never ridden a pony before. She hated to agree with Gina, but maybe she should look for a quieter, older animal to begin with.

At that moment Gina came up, her fluffy hair puffing out all round her crash hat. 'Your pony's down there at the end of the line,' she said sharply. 'I'm having this one.'

Emma glanced down to the end of the line. Gina was pointing to a black and white pony that was smaller than the others and looked as if it was already asleep. It was standing on three legs and leaning against the rail.

No way! thought Emma. 'This one's mine,' she said firmly, grabbing the chestnut pony's reins.

'Oh no it's not. You're having the dozy one at the end!' Gina hissed spitefully, and tried to prise Emma's hands away.

'What's going on, girls?' asked Graham, seeing the struggle.

'I've chosen this pony,' Emma said quickly, 'but Gina's trying to make me have the one at the end.'

'I *have* to have this one,' fumed Gina. Graham put his hand on her shoulder.

'This is Sultan, and I saw Emma choose him first, Gina. You're going to have to ride Snowball, the one at the end of the line.'

'But I'm an experienced rider. I need a decent pony to ride!' she protested. 'Snowball's half-asleep.'

'It takes skill to ride a lazy pony,' Graham pointed out. 'I'm sure you'll be able to wake him up.' And he escorted Gina down to the end of the line.

Emma turned back to Sultan. The argument had excited him even more. He was looking very playful, and as she ducked under the rail and went round to his side, he licked her face. She laughed. He was lovely – but was he going to be too much for her to handle?

Once everyone was matched up with a pony, Graham and the other instructors came down the line helping everyone mount up. Jamie and Mina and the others all scrambled up quickly. Gina didn't have to wait to be shown what to do. Emma was the last to get aboard. She could feel everyone's eyes watching her as Graham held Sultan's reins.

'Put your foot in the stirrup,' he instructed. Emma did as she was told, but Sultan didn't help. He moved, and she had to hop after him. She could hear Gina snickering behind her. For a second, Emma was scared. If she wasn't careful she could make a real fool of herself here – and she'd never be allowed to forget it.

'It's all right,' Graham said reassuringly. 'Don't worry. Hold on to his mane and then bounce into the saddle on the count of three. One, two, three . . . '

And before she was sure what had happened, Emma found herself sitting proudly in the saddle, a foot in each stirrup, and the reins in her hands. Sultan bobbed his head, but it didn't worry her. He was just eager to go off and explore. She pulled the reins in gently, as Graham showed her, and felt him come under her control. It felt fine!

'Right everyone, let's go!' called one of the instructors. Emma gave Sultan a gentle nudge with her heels and he walked on behind the other ponies. Jamie walked alongside on his black pony with a white blaze on its forehead.

'It feels as if we're really high up, doesn't it?' he said a bit nervously to Emma as they set off. And then he began to laugh. 'Look at Gina!'

Emma turned to look. Snowball obviously didn't want to go on a trek. He'd put his head down and was eating the grass. Gina was sitting there kicking and shouting – and nothing was happening. Emma grinned at the sight. 'So much for the brilliant horsewoman,' she said with a laugh.

'Come on Gina!' everyone shouted as Snowball ambled back into the paddock. Gina sat on his back kicking and smacking him, trying to get him

88

to trot or even just walk a little faster, but he ignored her efforts. The other ponies, including Sultan, lined up by the rail.

'We're going to dismount and then unsaddle our ponies,' Graham announced. 'Hold your reins like this,' he said, showing them how to dismount, 'then lift your leg over and jump to the ground like this.' He jumped.

Emma gulped. Graham made it look really easy, but she was sure it wouldn't be. She'd have to be careful not to put too much weight on her bad leg as she hit the ground.

'Stand still, Sultan,' she whispered to her pony. His ears flicked back as she spoke. He'd behaved himself perfectly all the way round the trail, unlike Snowball who'd lagged behind and held everyone up. Emma took her right leg out of the stirrup and swung it over Sultan's rump. For a second she swung there nervously, then gathered her courage and jumped. As she reached the ground her bad leg buckled at the knee and Emma fell down with a thump on her bottom. For a second she sat there feeling dazed.

'Oh dear!' came Gina Galloway's scathing voice. She jumped lightly down from Snowball. 'Had an accident, have we? What a surprise!'

'Are you okay?' Jamie offered a hand to help Emma up.

'Ouch!' she grimaced as she got to her feet and rubbed her hip. It felt sore. For a minute she was badly worried, but there didn't seem to be anything seriously wrong. Maybe her limp was a little bit worse when she walked, but there was nothing too painful.

Even so, Emma felt shaken. She couldn't remember the last time she'd fallen so heavily. Suddenly it was as if all the old fears from her younger days, when her leg was so much weaker, came flooding back.

If she'd landed just a little harder, something might have snapped. All the hard work done by the doctors might have been ruined. She could have found herself back on sticks again – and it would be her own fault. All the confidence she'd been feeling melted away into doubt and fear. What was she playing at, doing something as risky as riding?

'Don't you think you'd better forget about this afternoon's activities?' Gina said loudly. It was as if she could read Emma's thoughts. 'After all, riding is the easiest of all the things we're doing. How are you going to cope with the rock climbing after lunch?'

'I don't know,' Emma snapped angrily. Right now, she really wouldn't have minded passing up the rock climbing. When the group had been asked to vote for the activities they wanted to try, she and Mina had given the thumbs down to rock climbing. Unfortunately the others had wanted to do it and the vote had gone against them.

'Don't worry, you won't have to do it if you really don't want to,' Graham had assured them. But that had made Emma determined to give it a chance. And Gina's taunt made her feel even more determined. Gina was just like her parents, trying to convince her she wasn't able to do things. Though Emma had her own doubts, it made her blood boil to have someone else treat her like a child.

She tried to concentrate on Graham's instructions for taking off the pony's saddle, but somehow her mind kept wandering. How was she supposed to shorten the stirrups? Which buckle did she undo first? She couldn't move any of them.

'What do you do?' she asked Jamie.

'I'm not sure.' He was having trouble too. 'I can't even find the buckles!'

'I'll show you.' Gina pushed her way past Sultan's side, making it sound as if she was talking to a little child. 'It's simple.' She gave the girth strap a really sharp tug that made Sultan snort and sidestep. 'Shut up!' She gave him a hard smack on the flank. Emma saw him put his ears back.

'You just undo this,' Gina said patronisingly, giving the strap another yank. The saddle began to slip and Emma reached up and took it off.

'See, it's easy when you know how,' said Gina. She gave Sultan another hard slap on the flank. His ears flicked back again.

'Careful,' warned Emma. 'He doesn't like that.'

'He loves it. You don't know anything about horses.' Gina tapped him again. This time Sultan stepped backwards a couple of paces – right onto Gina's foot. She cried out in pain.

Emma grabbed the reins and pulled Sultan forward. Gina was hopping about, holding her toes and groaning.

'Poor Gina,' said Emma, trying not to smile too much. 'Have you hurt yourself?'

Gina muttered something. Emma wasn't sure if it was yes or no. 'Well,' she suggested, putting on the kind of concerned voice Gina had used for her, 'if it's painful you can sit out the rock climbing this afternoon. You can watch me have a go instead.'

Jamie and Mina had their hands clamped over their mouths, so as not to laugh too loudly. 'I'll manage it, thank you,' said Gina through gritted teeth. 'Don't worry, Emma. I'll show you . . .'

'You should have seen Gina's face!' Emma burst out laughing when everyone had returned to the adventure centre at five o'clock. They'd had showers and changed, ready for the evening events. Now they were gathered in the meeting room of the main building, waiting to find out what was coming next. 'She was mad! And she got even more angry when we went rock climbing. Jamie and Mina and I managed to get to the top of the cliff but she fell off only halfway up. She was on a rope, so she was all right – but boy, was she furious!'

'I wish I'd been there!' Jas's dark eyes were dancing with mischief.

'Me too,' chorused Liz and Charlie and Becky.

'We had a few disasters ourselves,' Liz said with a giggle. 'Jas thought she was the world's greatest canoeist until she tried shooting a tiny rapid and fell in!'

'It wasn't tiny!' protested Jas. 'And I couldn't help it if the canoe capsized!'

'She kept bobbing up in the water and spluttering. We thought she was going to drown,' Becky continued. 'And then one of the instructors got out of his canoe and *walked* over to her. The water was only about eighteen inches deep!' They all laughed.

'Well at least we've got the beach barbecue to look forward to this evening.' Jas sighed. 'Miss Tyler said there would be dancing, too. Bet I can guess who Emma will be dancing with.'

'And I'll be there taking pictures so we'll all be able to remember what happened when we're safely back in Wetherton,' added Charlie, waving her camera.

Emma went pink. They must be expecting her to dance with Jamie Thompson! Fortunately, before they could go on about him, Graham and the other instructors came in and everyone was quiet.

'Graham is gorgeous,' whispered Becky, her blue eyes flashing. 'Take a photo of him, would you, Charlie?'

Liz looked at her disbelievingly. 'Becky, *behave!* He must be at least ten years older than you!'

'Tonight, as you know, we've got a treat in store for you – a beach barbecue,' Graham announced. There was a cheer. 'But before you can enjoy the food, we're going to set you a challenge.'

'Oh, no,' Jas groaned, chewing furiously on her gum. 'I've had more than enough challenges for one day.'

'You're going to have to use your initiative to find the barbecue yourselves,' Graham explained. 'We want to divide you into teams of three. Each team will be given a map and a compass and we'll set you off on a treasure hunt to find the right spot. There are four clues to follow and the first team to get to the barbecue will win a prize.'

'Forget the prize,' moaned Jas. 'Just take me there in the mini-bus instead. I can't walk any further

93

tonight – I won't be able to dance when we get there!'

'You'll make it,' Liz comforted as they all got up and went outside to where the maps and the first clue were being issued. Emma noticed that most of the others were carrying sweatshirts. She'd come out in just her short-sleeved T-shirt. It would be cold on the beach once the sun went down.

'I need a sweater,' she called to the others. 'I'm just going back to the cabin to get one. Wait for me.'

It took only a few minutes, but when Emma got back to the spot, everyone had gone except for two people, who stood there waiting and looking uncomfortable, Jamie and Gina. Her heart sank. Of all the people she didn't want to have to spend the evening with, it was Gina.

'Miss Tyler made the others divide into teams and go off,' explained Jamie, looking pretty miserable. 'She told us to wait for you.'

'You took your time,' Gina added meanly.

'Have we got the map and the first clue?' Emma asked. 'We ought to get started. Everyone else was going off in that direction.' She pointed down the path through the woods.

'Well, they've got it wrong,' Gina said crisply. She held out the map. 'I overheard the instructors talking about the barbecue. I didn't get it all, but I definitely heard them say they're going to be holding it at Silverlight.'

'Silverlight?' Jamie asked, puzzled.

'Here.' Gina stabbed a finger at the map. 'They must mean Silverlight Head.' She pointed to a spot along the coast. 'And the quickest way to get there is by going that way.' She pointed in the opposite direction to the way in which everyone else had gone. 'If we just head there in a straight line, instead of zig-zagging all over the place following the clues, we could get there first and win the prize.'

Emma looked at the map and the clue. 'I don't think so,' she said after a few seconds. 'For a start, if we just head straight for Silverlight Head, we'd have to cross this area here – and the marks on the map show it's a boggy area. And secondly, the first clue we've been given says *"Go to the spot where the fairies play"*. That must mean the fairy ring of toadstools we saw on this morning's walk. If we go straight there, we can pick up the next clue.'

Gina's grey eyes flashed with annoyance. 'But we're already miles behind everyone else, thanks to you! We'll trail in last – and you may be happy to do that, but I'm not.'

'I'd rather do it properly than cheat!' retorted Emma.

'It's not cheating, it's using my initiative,' snapped Gina. Don't be such an angel, Emma. Grow up.'

That made Emma really mad. 'I *am* grown up,' she replied, 'which is why *I'm* going to do this thing properly. Are you coming with me?'

'No.' Gina handed her the map. 'I know exactly where I'm going. I'm going to forget all about the clues and make a straight line across the fields to Silverlight Head. And when you arrive in about three hours' time and miss the barbecue, I'll have a good laugh.' Gina's cotton-wool hair bobbed about in agitation. There were little spots of red on each of her cheeks that made her look like a china doll.

'Don't try it, Gina.' Jamie had been standing there, silently watching them. 'You don't know if you can actually get across those fields. There might be ditches or hazards that aren't on the map. There might be a bull!'

'Yes,' agreed Emma, though privately the thought of Gina being chased by a bull didn't bother her too much. 'That's probably why they've sent us round a longer way.'

Gina looked at them with disgust. 'You're a pair of real wallies,' she said scathingly. '*You* go the long way round if you want. I'm taking the shortcut.' And with that she set off. Emma watched her, feeling angry and worried, too.

'Maybe we ought to go with her in case she gets lost,' Jamie suggested.

Emma wrinkled her nose. 'I really want to do it properly, though. Why can't she just follow the rules for once?'

'Because she's Gina Galloway and she doesn't believe the rules apply to her.' Jamie raised an eyebrow. 'She shouldn't really be going off on her own without a map, you know. I'm not exactly her best friend, but I don't want her to get hurt, either.'

'I know.' Emma *was* worried, even though she disliked Gina so much.

Jamie frowned. 'Look, you've got the map and you know what you're doing. Why don't you follow the clues and I'll follow Gina, just to make sure she's okay.'

Emma nodded. She didn't mind following the trail on her own. And she'd prefer to do the whole challenge, rather than just walk across the fields. All the same, she wasn't very happy at the thought of Jamie following Gina. She'd have liked him to come with her. Trust Gina to manage to ruin everything. 'I'll see you at the barbecue,' was all she said.

'Yeah.' Jamie gave her his usual lopsided smile. 'See you later.' He ran off after Gina, who was disappearing in the distance.

Emma turned to go in the opposite direction. She knew just where she was going – and she was going to do it all on her own!

9

The first clue was easy. Emma just followed the path they'd taken that morning until she came to the fairy ring of toadstools. Some of the toadstools had been trampled down, but Emma still recognised the spot. In the centre of the ring was the second clue, written on a sheet of paper fastened to the ground. *'Use your ears to find the river, then step on it,'* she read.

She did what it said and stood absolutely still, listening. Through the rustling leaves she heard the sound of water trickling along. That must be what the clue meant! Emma began to make her way through the undergrowth in the direction of the noise. It didn't bother her, being alone in the countryside like this. She knew that the other kids weren't far ahead of her along the trail. In fact if they stopped to argue over the clues, she might soon catch them up.

Emma came out of the trees and saw the stream sparkling as it ran across the bottom of the small hill at the edge of the wood. And she could see the third clue in its yellow plastic bag, on the far bank.

But how was she going to get across to it? The stream was too wide to jump and according to the map, there was no bridge. What had that last clue said? *'Step on it.'* What did they mean by that? Emma was just about to take her shoes and socks off and wade across when she saw the stepping stones.

It was tricky getting across. The stones were slippery and wet and she was scared she'd fall in and get soaked. At one point, halfway across, she lurched unexpectedly and one foot shot into the water. But it was only her trainer that got wet, and she made it to the other side in safety. Her heart was beating like a drum in her chest and her knees felt weak, but apart from that she was fine. She'd done it – and all on her own, too!

For a second Emma wished that Jamie had been there to see her do it. She wanted a witness, someone who'd tell everyone else that she'd managed it all by herself, without any help. That would teach Gina that she didn't need babying!

The next clue was much easier. All Emma had to do was follow the footpath round the next field and head for the lighthouse she could see in the distance. Every now and then she spotted Clinton Walsh's figure bobbing up behind the hedge as he and the others in his team followed the route. His team weren't far ahead. It made Emma feel better to know that though she might be last to the barbecue, she wasn't going to arrive much behind the others.

The adventure centre's mini-buses were parked by the lighthouse so Emma guessed she didn't have far to go. Attached to one of the windscreens was another clue, which led her down the path to the cliff. From there it was a short scramble down to the beach.

Emma took her time. She hadn't minded rock climbing this afternoon because she'd been wearing a harness. It was a bit different going down the rocky path without one. She had no intention of tripping up and making a fool of herself.

In the distance she could see figures gathered on the sand. That must be the class! She walked towards them. It was a beautiful scene, with the evening sun glittering across the water and the smell of salt in the air. Further along the beach the cliffs got higher and higher, until in the distance they were towering above the water like huge white walls.

'Emma!' Jas and Charlie were calling her. They came running across the sand in their bare feet. Charlie was wearing a long flowery skirt that kept flying up under her chin. 'Are you coming for a paddle?'

'You got here!' cried Liz, following at a more sedate pace in her printed shorts and trainers and carrying a can of cola. 'We waited for you, honest. We wanted you to be in one of our teams, but Miss Tyler sent us off without you.' She held out the cola. 'Here, we all get one of these – it's your prize for getting here safe and sound.'

Emma took the can. A long cool drink was just what she needed right now. 'Who won the challenge?' she asked. 'Was it you?'

'No,' Charlie laughed disgustedly. 'Ryan Bryson and his team ran all the way here and got in first. We practically had to carry Jas, so we had no chance.'

'I'm exhausted!' Jas protested, aiming a pretend punch at Charlie.

'Ryan's not so happy, either. All he won was an adventure centre sweatshirt,' giggled Liz. 'And now he and his team are too tired to enjoy the party.'

'Speaking of which, I hope they hurry up with

the barbecue,' said Jas, screwing up her face. 'I'm starving!'

While they waited for the barbecue to begin, the five of them lay on the beach in the sun, watching the seagulls diving into the waves. 'I'm really glad I came. It's lovely, isn't it?' murmured Becky, staring across the waves. 'And you know, the best thing about it is that I can't hear Gina Galloway bragging away in her horrible voice.'

'Isn't she here?' Liz searched the crowd on the beach.

'What did you do to her, Emma?' chuckled Charlie, who was retying one of the scarves she wore around her neck. 'You didn't shove her in the river and leave her there, did you?'

Emma told them what had happened. 'I couldn't stop her. She'd made up her mind to get to Silverlight Head by the short cut. I tried arguing, but she wouldn't take any notice. Jamie went with her in case she got into trouble on her own.'

'Silverlight Head?' Liz looked puzzled. 'Why did she want to go there?'

'For the barbecue, of course!' Emma laughed. 'This is Silverlight Head.'

'No it's not.' Charlie pushed her glasses back up her nose. 'This is Silverlight Bay. It's on the map. Look.' She pulled a creased-up copy of the map out of her pocket. 'See? We came out of the woods here, across the river and along the footpath to the lighthouse.'

Emma looked out along the line of cliffs that disappeared around the corner into the next bay. 'So where's Silverlight Head?'

101

Charlie and Liz peered at the map. 'It's here. And that would be . . . ' Liz pointed northwards along the cliffs. 'Back there quite some way.' The cliffs were huge and grey where her finger was aimed.

'Trust Gina to take a ten-mile short cut!' laughed Jas. 'She's going to go crazy when she realises she's made a mistake.'

'She said she heard the instructors talking about having the barbecue at somewhere called Silverlight,' Emma explained. 'She must have looked on the map and immediately saw Silverlight Head. She didn't bother to look a bit further along the coast for Silverlight Bay.'

'Look at this,' said Charlie, pointing to the map again. 'These markings at Silverlight Head show seriously rocky cliffs. It doesn't look like a good place to go climbing around, if you ask me.'

Emma stared at the map. Charlie was right. It was difficult to tell just from the map, but Silverlight Head didn't seem to be a very friendly sort of place. 'What shall I do?' she wondered aloud.

'You'd better tell Miss Tyler,' Liz said firmly.

'But she'll go crazy if she finds out what Gina's done – and she'll be angry with me, too, for coming along the trail all on my own. You know we were supposed to stick together,' argued Emma.

Charlie and Jas were frowning. 'It's not your fault Gina's a cheat,' said Charlie. 'I think Miss Tyler should know.'

'There she is.' Becky pointed to where Miss Tyler was joining in the volleyball tournament. 'You'd better go and tell her now, Emma.'

*

'Okay, which way did they go?' Graham and Jane, one of the other instructors, picked up their ropes and put on the backpacks containing the rescue equipment. It all looked really serious. Emma hoped it wasn't going to be needed.

She'd come back to the adventure centre with Miss Tyler and the instructors to start looking for Gina and Jamie. Another group of searchers had set off along the beach to see if they could find the missing pair, but Graham had asked Emma to show him exactly which direction Gina had gone off in.

'They went down here. They were going to go in a straight line across all the fields.' Emma's feet were beginning to ache, but she ignored them as she headed in the direction that Gina had taken. They opened the gate and went across the field. There was no exit on the far side.

'They can't have come through here,' Miss Tyler said, looking for a gap in the fence. 'They must have gone back the proper way.' She was looking unusually tight-lipped. Emma could tell she was worried.

'No, look!' Emma's sharp eyes had spotted a scrap of yellow fabric caught on the cross-bar of the fence. Gina had been wearing baggy yellow shorts and from the look of it she'd torn them.

'Well done.' Graham helped Emma and Miss Tyler up, then he and Jane scrambled over.

The next field was like a swamp. They had to jump from one clump of grass to the next, trying to stay out of the mud.

'Oh no!' cried Miss Tyler as she stepped into it almost up to her knee. As she pulled her foot out, there was a slurping noise and her red trainer was left behind. Emma managed to grab it before it sank, but she was covered in slimy, sticky mud up to her elbow.

It took ages to cross the field and jump the stream on the far side. Then they climbed a steep hill. None of the adults talked much, except to discuss where Gina and Jamie might have gone. 'You really needn't come with us, Emma,' said Miss Tyler when they reached the top of the hill and tried to get their breath back. 'It might be too much for you.'

'But I want to come,' insisted Emma. It was true that her legs were aching and she felt tired, but she wasn't exhausted. She'd rather help look for Jamie and Gina than sit at the barbecue waiting to hear what had happened. She realised that she'd hardly given her leg a second thought in the last hour or so. It didn't seem to matter any more. She was just like everyone else, limp or no limp.

They walked carefully down the other side of the hill. The light was beginning to fade and they had to take care not to step in any rabbit holes. There was just one more field to cross before they reached the edge of the cliffs.

Charlie had been right, Emma thought as she stood well back and peered over. The cliffs at Silverlight Bay hadn't been very high or steep, but these dropped down almost sheer to the beach fifty yards below. The wind was much stronger here, too. A sudden gust caught them and Emma felt for a second as if she was in danger of being blown over the edge. Miss Tyler might have felt it too, because she stood well back. 'I've never had much of a head for heights,' she confessed. 'Surely they can't have tried to climb down here?'

'I wouldn't put it past Gina,' said Emma. She, too, wasn't very keen on looking over the edge. Not without a harness and a rope, anyway.

Graham, who'd been taking a closer look, came back. 'They must have walked that way,' he said pointing to the left. 'They couldn't go anywhere else.'

But for some reason Emma didn't feel so sure about that. She didn't know why, but she couldn't take her eye off a small mound of rocks on the cliff edge in the other direction. While Miss Tyler followed Graham, Emma went to check them out. 'Jamie!' she called. 'Gina!' Did she hear a very faint sound coming from the cliff?

'Emma! Stick with us!' Miss Tyler was standing waiting for her. 'This way. We don't want to lose you, too.'

'They might be up here,' Emma called, but Miss Tyler didn't seem to hear. The wind was in the wrong direction, Emma realised.

She called Jamie's name again. And again, though her ears could hardly make it out, she thought she heard something. The rocks by the edge of the cliff were loose and crumbly. Normally Emma wouldn't have gone near them. But this might be an emergency. And anyway, she'd managed okay at rock climbing this afternoon, hadn't she?

She inched nearer the edge. 'Jamie?' This time she definitely heard a shout. 'Miss Tyler! Graham! They're here!' she called as loudly as she could. Bit by bit she inched down the cliff. It was pretty dark now, so she had to guide herself by touch rather than sight.

Her fingers found tufts of grass and bits of flint embedded in the cliff face, and she clung tightly on to them as she moved each foot. 'Jamie?'

'Emma?' She heard him off to her right and began to move in that direction. There was a chunk of rock sticking out. She could stand on that. She put her right foot on it – and the rock broke away and fell with a crash to the beach below. Emma could feel her heart pounding fit to burst inside. Her fingers grabbed at anything they could find and she managed to hold on.

'Careful!' Jamie's white face was just visible a little below her on the right. 'Are you okay?'

'Whew!' Emma could hardly breathe. 'Yeah, I think so. How about you?'

'We're on a ledge, but we can't climb up again. Gina slipped and hurt herself. I think she's broken her arm.'

Out of the darkness came a whine. 'Who is it?'

'It's Emma. She's come to rescue us,' Jamie said calmly.

'Emma Pennington?' Gina couldn't have sounded more surprised if she'd tried. 'I don't believe it – but I don't care. Just get me out of here!' And she began to wail.

Emma felt like wailing too. She was stuck! She couldn't move to the right or the left without falling off the cliff. What were they all going to do?

At that moment a shower of tiny stones came tumbling down the cliff above her. Graham's feet appeared above her head and he came climbing down beside her, with a rope attached to the harness he'd put on. 'It's okay!' he said with a reassuring smile as he stopped by her and began to wrap the rope securely around her.

'Am I pleased to see you,' she said, almost laughing with relief.

Graham hung on to her. 'You've done your part of the rescue, Emma,' he said. 'Now it's my turn.'

'Gina was lucky just to break her arm if you ask me.' Liz shuddered as she brushed her hair. She was sitting on the edge of Emma's bed, dressed in a neat pink and white spotted dressing-gown. 'You might have been killed trying to find her, Emma.'

'And I can't believe that before they took her away in the ambulance she yelled at you for taking so long to rescue her!' Jas shook her head in amazement. 'Didn't she even thank you?'

'I expect she was in shock,' Emma said calmly.

'Will they keep her in there for long?' Jas, in her short black nightshirt, settled on the bed by Liz.

'Graham thought they'd probably let her come home on the bus with us tomorrow,' Emma explained with a yawn.

Charlie came in from the washroom, carrying her toothbrush. 'Well I don't know how you did it,' she said admiringly. 'I would just have passed out. You must have nerves of steel, Emma.'

'I don't know how you did it either.' Liz's arm tightened around Emma's shoulders. 'You're a heroine, you realise that?'

'If it wasn't for you, Gina and Jamie would have been stuck out on that ledge all night – or worse,' Becky added grimly. 'Miss Tyler and the instructors were heading in the opposite direction. They would never have found them.'

Emma shrugged and almost spilled her hot chocolate. She was sitting in her bunk in the dorm, after a long, hot shower. She felt exhausted, but also strangely calm and happy. 'I don't feel very brave,' she said softly. 'I was scared stiff. And you're forgetting how brave Jamie was, trying to save Gina in the first place. I knew Graham and Miss Tyler were nearby, but he tried it all on his own.'

Liz nodded. 'I saw him coming back to camp. He looked okay, apart from a black eye.' Emma felt relieved to hear that.

'I can't believe Gina!' Becky shook her head. 'She's just so dumb.'

'And you want to hear something really funny?' asked Charlie, wrapping her quilt around her shoulders as she sat on the bunk opposite. 'Gina told me that it would be bad news if Emma came on this trip, because we'd have to look after her!'

'I don't believe it!' Jas shrieked. 'And just look what's happened. You're the one who's rescued *her*!'

'Just let her try telling me I'm a baby now!' Emma chuckled wickedly, with a gleam in her eye. 'She's never going to say one mean word to me again.'

Liz laughed, but sat staring at Emma with an amazed expression. 'I can't believe this is the same Emma who wouldn't have said boo to a goose a few weeks ago. That Emma didn't even do gym, let alone rescue people from cliffs! It's incredible.'

'Yeah, you're not the angel we used to know – you're much better now,' added Jas.

Charlie winked meaningfully and said with a grin,

'And they don't know just how bad you've really been, do they, Emma?'

'No!' Emma smiled ruefully.

'What's going on?' Jas tugged at her toes through the bedcover. 'Come on, no secrets.'

Emma hesitated for a second. She could trust the others, she was sure. They were her friends. They'd support her. 'My parents think I'm spending the weekend with Charlie – back in Wetherton,' she explained.

'You mean they don't know you're here?' Becky's mouth fell open. 'But what about that signature on your form?'

'My aunt's – and it was forged,' Emma confessed. Jas and Becky's eyes opened so wide, she thought they'd pop out of their sockets.

'Wow!' squeaked Jas.

'You mean they didn't change their minds about you coming on this trip?' asked Liz, unable to believe what she'd just heard.

'No,' nodded Emma. 'They wouldn't let me. They said it was too risky.'

'Good job you did come,' commented Charlie, braiding her hair. 'Otherwise Gina and Jamie might still be out there, clinging to a cliff.'

'But what are you going to tell them when you get back?' Liz wanted to know. 'They'll go crazy when they find out what's happened.'

Emma took a big gulp of hot chocolate. 'If we get back on time they'll never know,' she said more cheerfully than she felt deep down.

'But they're bound to hear about what happened,' insisted Liz. 'It'll be all round the school by Monday morning and someone's mum will bump into yours and say something about you rescuing Gina.'

Emma smiled ruefully. She hadn't thought about that. Liz was right. It was impossible to keep a secret at Bell Street. News always got round.

'Well we think you're a heroine,' said Becky, patting Emma on the back.

'Maybe,' murmured Emma. 'But I don't think my parents will agree . . .'

10

'What's the time?' Emma asked for the hundredth time. The coach turned right into Bell Street. In two minutes they'd be back at the school and she'd know exactly what fate had in store for her.

'Twenty to seven.' Charlie looked tense, too. 'It's well past your family's tea time, isn't it?'

'Yes.' Emma nodded grimly. She settled herself back in her seat and prepared for the worst. They were two hours late. There had been a delay while they waited for Gina to be brought back to the adventure centre from the hospital, her arm in plaster. And then it had been nothing but traffic jams all the way home. Emma gritted her teeth. She must have been mad to think she could go on the trip and not get into trouble for it.

The coach swung into the school drive. It was lined with cars and parents, all waiting to collect their children. 'Uh-oh.' Charlie nodded towards the entrance. Her dad was standing on the school steps with Mr and Mrs Pennington at his side. All three of them were grim-faced.

'They've found out that I was covering for you,' muttered Charlie, pushing her glasses back up her nose. 'Now I'm going to be for the chop, too.'

'I'm sorry, Charlie. I hope you don't get into

too much trouble,' Emma whispered as the coach reversed into position. 'Tell your mum and dad I talked you into helping me out.'

'I'll be okay.' Charlie grinned. 'It's *you* I'm worried about.'

Emma felt pretty worried, too. Her stomach had suddenly started doing backflips and her legs felt weak and trembly. She didn't want to get off the coach and face the music – but she didn't have any choice.

Becky and the others turned round in their seats. 'Good luck,' they said quietly.

'I'm going to need it.' Emma gulped.

Gina, tears streaming down her cheeks, was being let off the bus first. Miss Tyler had the job of explaining her injury to her parents. Jamie, with his eye all battered, was the next off, assisted by another teacher.

'Remember you're a heroine,' called Becky as she jumped down the steps from the bus.

As Emma followed her, her father's hand fell heavily on her shoulder. 'Hello, Dad,' she said as brightly as she could, but he looked grey and stern.

'We're going straight home, Emma.' His voice sounded icy. 'And then you're going to tell us just what's been going on.'

'How could you do it?' Mrs Pennington shut her eyes in disbelief. 'After everything we've done for you, Emma, how could you disobey us like this?' She blew her nose on her handkerchief.

'We've been worried all day, since the moment we found out that you hadn't spent the weekend at the

Farrels'.' Her father was standing at the fireplace, one hand on the mantelpiece.

'You wouldn't let me do anything – not even perfectly safe, sensible things like swimming or riding a bike.' Emma folded her arms defensively. She wasn't going to cave in and admit defeat. 'You've protected me for too long. What was I supposed to do? I had to prove I'm just like everybody else.'

'But you're not!' her mother protested.

'I am!' Emma insisted. 'I've proved it this weekend. I did everything the others did and I'm fine. I even helped rescue—'

'We don't want to hear about what you've been doing,' snapped her father. 'The fact is, you disobeyed us.'

There was a loud clunk outside the living-room door, but no one except Emma seemed to hear it. 'We told you we didn't approve of you going on this weekend, but despite that you sneaked and schemed your way on to it. You told us lies. We're very disappointed in you.'

Emma stuck her chin in the air. 'I wish I hadn't had to do all that,' she said firmly, 'but I don't regret a single thing. If you didn't treat me like a little kid, I wouldn't have had to go behind your backs.'

Both her parents looked shocked. 'I don't know what's got into you!' cried Mrs Pennington. 'What's made you change so suddenly? You never used to be any trouble, but now you do nothing but argue and misbehave.'

'I'm just growing up,' Emma said flatly, beginning to get bored with the arguments.

113

Her father put his head on one side. 'Maybe,' he murmured. 'But you have to learn to behave like an adult – and lying and deceiving people are not acceptable forms of behaviour. So to make sure you learn your lesson, we're grounding you.'

'For how long?' Emma had expected it. Everybody got grounded sooner or later. Getting grounded was a mark of growing up.

'A month. And if we're not satisfied with your behaviour after that, another month. And if necessary—'

'It's all right, I get the picture,' Emma said sullenly. She could feel her lower lip beginning to tremble ever so slightly, but she wasn't going to let them see how she felt. Rebels didn't burst into tears when they got caught.

'And you're not going to the school disco,' Mrs Pennington added with a deep breath.

Emma gulped. That really did hurt. Grounding wasn't so bad. After all, it wasn't as if she was out every night of the week having a great time. But the disco – that was something special. 'Is that all?' she asked in a wobbly voice.

Her parents nodded. 'You can go straight to your room,' said Mrs Pennington. 'You're going to school tomorrow.'

Emma went to the door and turned the handle. 'I'm not sorry about anything,' she said defiantly as she went out into the hall.

Aunt Ed was standing at the bottom of the stairs with a big grin on her face. As Emma emerged from the living-room she punched the air victoriously and uttered a silent 'Yes!' Her plaster cast clunked as she

114

climbed the stairs. Emma grinned. She guessed Aunt Ed had been listening at the door.

Up on the landing, Andrew opened his door and peered out at the two of them. 'What have you done?' he asked, amazed. 'It's been like World War Three here since Mum and Dad got back.'

'I'll tell you all about it tomorrow,' Emma said wearily. Right now she couldn't face any more questions.

Later, when she'd had a bath and got into bed, Aunt Ed came tapping on the door of her room. 'Don't look so miserable,' she said cheerfully. 'They'll get over it. Parents always do.'

Emma smiled sleepily. 'You reckon?' She had her doubts. What if she was grounded for ever?

'I promise.' Aunt Ed stroked her hair. 'The most important thing is whether you had a good time or not.'

'I had a great time, the best time ever.' She wanted to tell Aunt Ed all about it – but right now she could hardly keep her eyes open.

'What else matters then?' asked Aunt Ed, snuggling up. She was wearing another fluffy sweater, this time in a tartan pattern, and she felt very cosy and warm. Emma was glad she was there. 'Growing up means accepting the bad times as well as the good. You had a great weekend and now you're grounded. But you'll live, and there'll be lots of good times in the future.'

'Yeah, you're right.' Emma smiled to herself. 'I'm really glad you're here, Aunt Ed,' she murmured, just before she fell asleep.

*

115

'It's not fair!' Charlie gritted her teeth. 'Can't they see how unreasonable they're being? My parents have grounded me for going along with your scheme for the trip to Wales, but only for a week. That's fair enough.'

Emma laughed. 'That's just it. My parents think they're being really fair!'

Liz picked a tuft of grass and threw the bits in the air. 'I wish there was something we could do to make them see how wrong they are.' The girls were sitting on the grassy bank on the edge of the playing field. Behind them was the playground and behind that the main modern block of the school.

'There's nothing,' Emma said, sighing. 'I'm grounded and banned from the disco and that's that. Oh,' she remembered, '*and* my mum's confiscated my leggings.'

'I don't believe it!' Becky held her blond head in her hands. 'Everybody wears leggings! My step-mum wears them and she's thirty-five years old!'

'Why are your parents so old-fashioned?' asked Jas, smoothing down her black mini-skirt.

'I don't know.' Emma shrugged. 'Maybe they were just born that way. It's impossible to believe they were ever young.'

'I just think they don't want you to grow up. They're scared they'll lose you. They want you to stay their little darling for ever and ever,' said Becky, giggling. 'Even when you're old and grey!'

'You're probably right.' Emma nodded seriously. It really felt as if her parents were trying to hang on to their little girl. The problem was, she wasn't that little girl any more. Somewhere, somehow, without really

116

noticing what was happening, she'd grown up. But how long would it take before they realised that, too?

Jamie was waiting for Emma as she came out of the dining hall after lunch. 'Hi,' he said shyly. His eye was bruised and swollen, but otherwise he was fine.

'Becky told me your parents have banned you from the school disco.' He gave her that slightly lopsided look.

'Yes.' Emma nodded gloomily. 'And I'm grounded until I turn back into a good girl again.'

Jamie looked disappointed. 'I was going to ask if you'd come to the disco with me,' he murmured, adding quickly. 'Not just because you came to the rescue at the weekend. I was going to ask you before that, too.'

Emma watched him redden and felt herself go a matching colour. 'I'd really like to come.' She sighed. 'But I can't. They're dead set against it. And I don't plan to turn back into a good girl. I may never be allowed out again.' She raised one eyebrow and they both giggled.

It was strange. A couple of weeks ago she would have laughed at the idea of having Jamie as a boyfriend, but now she really liked him. She didn't want one of the flashy older boys everyone else was crazy about. She had much more in common with someone like Jamie.

Other people seemed to feel the same way all of a sudden. The school was buzzing with the story of how Jamie had tried to rescue Gina. Now all the people who'd ignored him wanted to talk to him and admire his black eye.

117

Emma knew she should be pleased about it for his sake, but the thought of Jamie going to the disco with another girl was hard to bear.

He frowned. 'Can't you make your parents change their minds?'

Emma laughed. 'How? Just tell me and I'll do it.'

He stared at her with his deep brown eyes. The bruised one wouldn't open properly and made him look battered and cute. 'I don't know,' he muttered. 'But if I think of something, I'll let you know.'

'Thanks.' Emma felt near to tears. Everyone was being so sympathetic, and somehow it made things worse. She didn't want to cry, so she changed the subject. 'What did your parents say about your black eye? Were they angry?'

'No!' He laughed. 'My dad's really proud of it. He thought I'd got it in a fight. I told you my parents have some pretty strange ideas.'

'Well, they're right to feel proud of you,' Emma reminded him. 'you climbed down to that ledge to make sure Gina was okay.'

'But if you hadn't come along to rescue the pair of us, that might have been it,' he insisted. 'And I didn't climb down that cliff in the dark.' He suddenly stopped. 'Hey, I have an idea.'

'What?' asked Emma.

He shook his head. 'I'm not going to tell you. Just wait and see.'

'Emma?' Aunt Ed came clunking down the hall-way as soon as Emma opened the front door that afternoon. Before Emma had time to put down her school bag, she asked, 'Tell me, did you get a package from Australia? It should have arrived while I was away.'

Emma was puzzled for a second, then she remembered. 'Yes, something was delivered last Friday morning, I think. Mum mentioned it. She didn't say it was from Australia, though. I was in so much of a hurry to get away I didn't look at it.'

'Then we've got to find it!' Aunt Ed said excitedly. 'It may be more important than you think.'

They didn't have to look far. Her father must have decided to put it in a safe place because it was on the top shelf of the dresser. Emma scrambled up on a chair to get it down. 'Careful,' said Aunt Ed, holding the chair.

Emma tried not to laugh. Once you'd climbed down a cliff in the dark, getting up on a kitchen chair hardly seemed dangerous. She handed the parcel to Aunt Ed. It felt like a thick, heavy book.

'Wonderful. Now let's go up to my room and see what we've got,' Aunt Ed said mysteriously.

'How do you know what's in it?' Emma asked, not understanding what was going on.

'Remember that letter you posted to my daughter in Australia?' Aunt Ed raised an eyebrow.

'Yes.' Emma nodded. It felt like ages ago.

'Well, I asked her to send you this because I thought it might be useful.' Aunt Ed smiled wickedly. 'And you know, I think it might have arrived at a very good time.'

'Mum, Dad, don't leave the table yet – I've got something really interesting to show you.'

Emma's father looked at her warily, as if he didn't trust her – but he didn't get up from the supper table, either. Emma reached under her chair and pulled out the package. The brown wrapping paper was just loosely folded around it and she unwrapped it, revealing a battered old photo album.

'Look what Aunt Ed's lent me,' Emma said cheerfully. 'It's full of surprises, you know.' Aunt Ed sat back in her chair and just smiled, as if the photo album really had nothing to do with her.

Emma opened the album at a page showing a young man climbing a lamp-post. He was dangling from the top and grinning for the camera. 'I wonder who this is?' she asked. 'Aunt Ed says it's you, Dad, but I can't believe you ever climbed a lamp-post.'

Andrew leaned across the table and pulled the album in his direction. 'Let's have a look. Hey! Dad, it *is* you!' He roared with laughter. 'Don't you look silly!'

'Edna!' snapped Mr Pennington, going bright pink as he stared at the picture, 'what's going on?'

Aunt Ed just held out her hands innocently. 'I could see Emma was having trouble believing that you'd ever been young and foolish, so I thought I'd prove to her once upon a time you did a few reckless things yourself.'

Emma turned on through the album. 'Here's another funny one,' she giggled. 'Look at the pair of you in this picture! Look, Dad, you've got a beard and you're wearing a kaftan and beads!'

Andrew was having hysterics. 'I thought it was a dress,' he gasped.

'Everyone wore kaftans in those days,' Mr Pennington rumbled, trying not to laugh at himself.

'And look at Mum in this mini-skirt!' Emma exclaimed.

It was Mrs Pennington's turn to gasp at the photo of herself in a white mini-skirt and matching knee-high boots.

'Wow, Mum!' Andrew wolf-whistled. 'Look at those legs! And you complained about Sally wearing a short skirt when she came home from college at Christmas!'

'It was fashionable in those days,' protested Mrs Pennington. 'Everyone wore short skirts.'

Aunt Ed nodded. 'Yes, I can remember showing my knees. I was considered quite daring. But not as daring as you, Marjorie. You were very fashionable. Do you remember wearing white lipstick and false eyelashes?'

'I hardly ever wore them,' said Mrs Pennington, looking flustered. 'And I don't remember my skirts being *that* short.'

'It *is* pretty short, Mum,' Emma commented, sounding as innocent as she could. 'Far more revealing than my leggings.'

Mrs Pennington frowned. 'Don't think I can't see what you're up to,' she muttered with a straight face.

Emma turned another page. There was a photo of seven young people squashed into an open-topped sports car. Her parents were clinging on to the back seat, laughing for the camera. 'That's a bit dangerous, isn't it?' she asked. 'You two took a few risks in your time, didn't you?'

But her parents didn't seem to be listening. 'Do

121

you remember that day, Phil?' asked her mum. 'We went down to the south coast . . . ' They gazed briefly at one another, remembering it all.

'Yes,' murmured Aunt Ed quietly, 'we were all much younger and less serious then.'

Emma turned another page. This time instead of a picture, there was a newspaper cutting. Local Boy Found Safe in London, it read.

'Edna, I can't believe you kept that!' Mr Pennington had risen from his chair, looking shocked.

'I've read all about it, Dad,' Emma told him. 'About how you ran away to London to see a rugby match because your father wouldn't let you go, and the police went looking for you. Aunt Ed told me you were a bit of a rebel in your time, but I didn't believe her to begin with.'

'I didn't know about this.' Mrs Pennington was reading the cutting. 'Phil, is this all true?'

Her father sucked in his breath and looked at Aunt Edna as if he didn't know whether to laugh or shout at her. 'Yes it's true,' he admitted. And then, with mock despair, 'Edna, why do you do these things to me!'

Aunt Edna laughed. 'Because I don't like watching you turn into an old fogey, Phil. You've been treating Emma as if you have no idea what it's like to be young and desperate to try new things. I just wanted her to know that you haven't always been so careful and serious.'

'But Edna,' protested Mrs Pennington. 'Emma's *our* daughter—'

'I know.' Aunt Ed nodded. 'And I'm just an interfering old aunt who has no right to tell you how to bring her up. Except that I'd like her to have some fun while she's young.'

Emma's parents looked at each other, but before they could say anything the front doorbell rang. 'Probably someone for me,' said Mr Pennington, walking down the hallway to answer it.

Emma listened to a low voice and the sound of footsteps coming into the house and going into her father's study. Then her father came back into the kitchen.

'It's Miss Tyler, Emma's form teacher, and Jamie Thompson, a boy from her class,' he said, looking and sounding completely puzzled. Emma looked up. What was Jamie up to? 'They've come to speak to us, Marjorie. They're waiting in my study.'

Mrs Pennington glanced at Emma. 'Did you know they were coming?'

'No,' said Emma. Her surprise must have shown on her face because Mrs Pennington got up and followed her husband down the hall.

'This is a turn up for the books,' commented Aunt Ed raising her eyebrows. 'I wonder what's going on now?'

Emma just shook her head in disbelief. She had no idea!

Emma and Aunt Ed were watching a TV quiz game and beating all the contestants hands down. 'We should go on that programme together, you and I,' said Aunt Ed. 'We could have had a washing machine, a holiday in Barbados and a cuddly polar bear by now!'

Emma giggled. She was only giving half her

concentration to the quiz. The other half was focused on her father's study. Aunt Ed had tried lingering in the hallway to listen to what was going on behind the door, but with no luck. Her parents seemed to have been in there together for ages since Jamie and Miss Tyler had left. It was a complete mystery.

The pair of them were just about to answer the questions for the star prize, a shining new car, when Mr Pennington came into the living-room and interrupted. 'Emma, your mum and I would like a few words, please.'

Aunt Ed gave her an encouraging wink as she got up and followed him to the study. Her mum was sitting in the comfy chair usually reserved for visitors. She looked happier than she had for some time. Her dad perched on the edge of his desk. His hair was all fluffy and standing on end, as if he'd been running his hands through it.

'Emma, this has been quite an evening. Your mum and I have had to do some serious thinking.' Mr Pennington coughed, as if what he had to say was going to be difficult. 'And we feel, on reflection, that perhaps we haven't been very fair to you.'

Emma felt a sudden surge of excitement and hope.

'Miss Tyler came to tell us how you'd helped to rescue Gina.' Mrs Pennington looked quite tearful as she talked. 'Why didn't you tell us what had happened?'

'I tried to, but you just cut me short,' Emma said with the simple truth. 'You didn't want to know about the things I'd done.'

Her mother nodded ruefully. 'When I saw Gina getting off the bus with her arm in plaster and

Jamie with his black eye, I was terrified. I was in no mood for hearing what you'd actually done over the weekend.'

'The thought of you clambering around on the cliffs at night is horrifying!' exclaimed her father. 'Do you realise what might have happened?'

'Yes,' said Emma flatly. 'But I'm okay, and so are Gina and Jamie. That's what really matters.'

Her parents nodded. 'And we're very proud of you,' admitted her father. 'We're proud of our brave daughter and shocked that the news had to come from a stranger. It's made us realise that there's some truth in what you've been saying for the past few weeks. Perhaps we have been over-protective towards you.'

'But only for your own good, Emma,' her mother said quickly. 'Or anyway, what we thought was your own good.'

'I know.' Emma nodded. 'I know you do your best for me, honestly.'

'Good.' Mrs Pennington smiled. 'Anyway, we've been talking and we've decided that perhaps it's time we start handing over some more decisions to you. We know you're sensible, despite all the problems that have happened recently.' She cleared her throat. 'So, if you would like to do gym class and other activities at school, we'll trust your judgement and try not to clip your wings.'

'Thank you!' Emma said quietly.

'It's difficult for us, this letting you go,' her father added. 'We'd really like to keep you safe and protected for ever – but we realise we can't do that.'

'I don't want to run away from you!' Emma exclaimed. She flung her arms round her mother's neck. 'I just want to be a bit more like the other girls.'

'We understand that.' Her mother gave her a big hug. 'And as the other girls are all going to the disco, and we think Jamie seems a very nice boy, we're going to allow you to go too.'

'That doesn't mean to say that we're not very disappointed about you sneaking off on the adventure trip,' insisted her father. He tried to look really stern, but Emma could see the crinkles at the corners of his eyes.

'I'm sorry I had to do it like that,' Emma said honestly, and kissed him. 'Thanks, Dad. I promise I won't do that again.'

And she really meant it.

'I don't believe it's you!' Becky squeaked. They were in the cloakroom at school. Outside in the hall the disco music was pounding away.

'It's me all right!' Emma grinned. 'What do you think?'

'I think that top is too gorgeous for words.' Becky reached out and stroked the apricot-coloured silky fabric. 'And all those little buttons. It's really neat.'

'My Aunt Ed bought it for me,' Emma explained. 'Gina Galloway's got one just like it. She threatened to wear it tonight but her plaster cast won't go through the sleeve!' The others laughed.

'And look,' said Jas, 'you're wearing eyeshadow! It really suits you.'

Emma blushed. 'Aunt Ed lent me some of hers.'

She felt really great in her new outfit, but she didn't want too much fuss made over her. 'You two look wonderful too,' she said. Becky was wearing a blue dress with a short skirt and vest top. Jas, as usual, was wearing black – black leggings and a shiny black overshirt. With her short hair, she looked really stylish.

'Have you seen Liz?' Emma asked.

'Not yet,' replied Jas. 'I don't know what's got into that girl.'

At that moment Charlie came bursting in in a flurry of bangles and beads and wild red hair.

'Look what I've got!' She waved a yellow envelope above their heads. 'Photos from the adventure weekend! And you should see some of them. I've got a brilliant shot of Becky yawning.' She began handing the pictures round and there was an explosion of giggles. The pictures were hilarious.

'Can I borrow them?' Emma asked seriously when they'd all been seen. 'Just so that my mum and dad can see what we really got up to over the weekend. I think they're still under the impression we spent all our time doing incredibly dangerous things.'

'Sure,' said Charlie. 'I wonder if Miss Tyler is here yet. I want to show her the one of her in her nightshirt.'

'And how about Jamie?' Jas wanted to know. 'He's probably waiting out there, terrified Emma's going to stand him up.'

'I really like Jamie,' Becky said. 'I used to think he was a bit creepy before, but once you get talking to him he's really nice.'

'Yeah, he's nice,' admitted Emma. 'I don't know

127

if I'll be brave enough to dance tonight, but we'll have a good time anyway.'

'You don't have to be brave to dance. You just move with the music, like this.' Jas began to dance and Emma watched admiringly. Dancing was another of those things she'd thought she couldn't do because of her leg. But like rock climbing and volleyball, perhaps it wasn't so difficult after all.

'I wonder where Liz is,' said Becky, looking at her watch. 'It's not like her to keep us waiting. She said she'd be here fifteen minutes ago.'

'She's never around when you need her these days. Have you noticed that?' Jas smoothed down her leggings. 'Maybe she's up to something. She keeps disappearing after school.'

'Maybe she's doing something secret,' mused Emma.

'A secret?' Jas laughed. 'Good old sensible Liz?' Then she suddenly looked serious. 'Well, if she has, I'd like to know what it is.'

'Me too,' nodded Becky. 'Shall we see if we can find out?'

Is Liz up to something? Find out in Mystery Boy, *the third book in the Bell Street School series.*